WRITTEN BY G. PRINCE

NOVEMBER 11, 2013

I.S.B.N. 978-0-9897486-1-2

GHETTO GAMES

II

The Ghetto Saga Continues

A deadly street tale of revenge,

drugs, murder, and betrayal told in it's

rawest form.

G. Prince

ISBN 978-0-9897486-1-2

Disclaimer

This is a work of absolute fiction. The author has invented and created all of the characters, dialog and incident are the product of the author's imagination. Any resemblance to actual persons life or lifestyle; living or dead, is purely coincidental

<u>Synopsis</u>

Game died and left his three young protégés Ty, Julian, and G-Fly, his wealth, businesses, territory and West Coast Drug Empire. The game couldn't be sweeter for the three youngsters, until a Compton drug Kingpin decides that he wanted to take over the territory that Game left behind. But Ty, Julian, and G-Fly has no intention on giving up their inheritance, which results in a bloody game of death in the coldest ghetto warfare to ever hit the streets of California.

The sequel continues, in the rawest story ever told, "Ghetto Games II" A triple platinum ghetto street novel that's action packed, and guaranteed to keep you lost in suspense in the scandalous ghetto streets of California.

Table of Contents

Chapter 1
Blood In and Blood Out

It was May of 1988 and Julian, Ty, and G-Fly were at their round table discussing the problems that had arisen. "Game," the three youngsters mentor died nine months ago and since then a lot of other gangsters and hustlers from all over was trying to take over as much of Games territory as they could. But the youngsters were far from being slow, and they would die in the heat of battle before they allow someone to take over the territory that they inherited.

G-Fly slammed his hand on the long black marble table where they were seated at and said, "I'm tired of these niggas around here taken pop shots at our workers and jackin our dope spots. We need to make an example of these niggas and do it quick, or else nobodies gonna respect us".

"I feel you G-Fly, but we can not be shooting up petty hustlers around town just because they getting money and trying to eat close to our other dope spots" Julian reasoned!

"Why not? They're shooting at our workers and robbing our spots….don't we suppose to have some sort of loyalty to even the smallest workers who pushing our dope blocks and dope houses?" G-Fly responded in an aggravated tone!

"Yes, to a degree that we will supply them with good products for a decent price. Only our immediate family members receive that kind of unlimited support."

"That's bullshit Julian," G-Fly argued!

"Listen G-Fly, we're moving 200 kilos a week and we don't even serve a muthafucka no more. Princess and the girls are the only ones who still distribute weight to our clients, and they don't sell less then 10 keys a pop. If it wasn't for Wheel's and his crews, then we wouldn't even provide weight to niggas who sell ounces and have rock houses."

"But Wheels is still part of our family," said G-Fly!

"Yeah but he's a distant cousin per-se! The girls give him 20 keys a week and he supplies his workers and rock houses. So if Wheels want to go to war over his territory then he needs to man up," Julian argued.

"Hold up! Game built his territory through his sweat and blood, and he gave his life for the empire that he left to us, and now you want to just let some other niggas come and take it from us? Hell naw, I'm not feeling that! Just because you're about to get married to Tracy in a couple of weeks, don't mean that you should neglect your gangsta obligations."

"What do me getting married to Tracy got to do with anything," Julian asked?

"Everything nigga, you're getting soft and baby got you pussy whipped!" G-Fly said.

"Fuck you Fly, ain't nothing soft about me nigga." Julian said as he jumped up from his chair and Ty jumped up and stood in between him and G-Fly.

"Hold up you guys, ya'll need to chill out!" Ty said as G-Fly and Julian looked at each other crazy then sat back down.

"Now listen, we're all in this shit together! As long as we're in this game, then we need to deal with the circumstances and problems with some sort of honor and integrity. Now G-Fly got a point, we need to defend our territory like the gangsta's that we are, and was raised to be. But, Julian also makes a valid point; we're pushing a lot of weight now, so we need to find a way to distant ourselves from the small dealers in the game, so we can become more untouchable."

"Listen man, I got more then the average nigga would make in a life time, and I'm thinking about walking away and letting you and G-Fly have the dope game, and I'll just keep the legitimate ventures together." Julian conveyed.

G-Fly jumped up and said, "I told you that this nigga was getting soft on us.... This niggas pussy wooped!"

Julian jumped up and grabbed G-Fly by the shirt and they started wrestling. They fell on the ground and Ty just reached over and lit a joint while he watched. They threw a couple of weak blows at each other while they wrestled and then G-Fly said, "Let me go nigga!"

"You let me go first!"

"Let go of my head nigga," G-Fly utter in-between breaths.

"Let go of my hair first," Julian said.

Ty got up and pried them both apart as G-Fly pulled off his shirt and Julian picked up his diamond Rolex chain off the rug. "You broke my shit nigga; you're going to buy me another one!" Julian said looking pissed off.

"I ain't buying you shit nigga, fuck that chain and your soft ass too!" G-Fly shouted.

Julian was about to rush G-Fly again but Ty jumped in-between them again, and said; "Hold up! Look at you two.. acting like little kids. You nigga's need a reality check because you guys is allowing this shit to come between ya'll. We came along way in this game,... from rags to riches, remember that? We vowed death before dishonored, and to always be

loyal to each other until death do us part! Now G-Fly
if your brother wants to take some time away from
this game to enjoy his soon to be wife and his little
baby when it arrive, then we got to respect that. It
might be good to have him watching over our
business investments while we're doing what we do
best. That doesn't make him soft or less loyal to us in
this game. Maybe you should think about taking
some time away when Lady-G has your little
gangsta'. I can deal with this shit while ya'll gone.
We're at a point now that we ain't got to get our
hands dirty, so we can play from a distant now."

"What about our territory then," G-Fly asked?

"We'll do some investigation and see who's
behind it and eliminate him. If we kill the head, then
the body will fall, and if not, then we'll just have to
kill the body too!" Ty said, as him and G-Fly laughed
and Julian just smiled and shook his head.

"You feel me," Ty asked G-Fly?

"Yeah I feel you big bro." G-Fly said as he gave
Ty dap!

"Well, I think that you owe your brother an
apology!" Ty said as he looked at Julian.

"I apologize J, you know that I got mad love for
Tracy man, but I just hate to see you leave the game
man. It won't be the same without you by our side....
We're the three Generals!" G-Fly emotionally stated.

"My nigga, I'ma always have your back when
you need me, but I just want to play the game from a
distant. You feel me? I ain't trippin off of my share;
ya'll can split that between you too. I just want to do
a little traveling with my lady and baby when he
comes, and see what the other way of life is all about.
You feel me?"

"Hell naw, but if that's what you choose, then I'ma respect it. And you can still keep your cut of the dope. Money can never come between us! G-Fly said as him and Julian gave each-other a ghetto embrace.

Lady-G knocked on the door and they knew that it had to be important for her to interrupt them.

"Come in....!" Ty called out.

Lady-G opened the door and said, "I apologize for interrupting you guys but I got Hector on the phone."

G-Fly eyes got big from the sound of their drug connection name. "Thank you baby," he said as he grabbed the phone from Lady-G and slapped her on her big pregnant ass as she said, "Ouch!" and smiled and closed the door as she walked out.

"Hello! Hey commo esta my friend." G-Fly said.

"Yes this line is clean. O'kay! Don't worry my friend, say no more.... I'm on my way. Give me three hours! O'kay! See you when I get their – later." G-Fly hung up and looked over at Ty and Julian and said, "We got a G-Red!"

"What's up Fly," Julian asked?

"Nigga ain't you backing up!" Julian's eyes got big then he sat back in his chair. "O'kay then make up your mind! Anyway Ty, Hector son Juan just got set up by an undercover police....but peep, the muthafucka was working for one of Juan's people, so Juan's locked up with no bail and his people is at a safe house hiding out. So Hector needs a different race to do the job so it won't look as if his people were involved."

"Damn, that don't sound too good! Do you want me to go," Ty asked?

"Naw, I got it! You just take care of things around here and tell Princess and them that I said to be extra careful and cautious out there. I got a funny feeling about this territorial war shit." G-Fly said as he stood up and gave Ty and Julian a ghetto embrace and walked out of the room.

"Ty looked over at Julian with his eyes bucked and Julian shook his head and grabbed the indo joint and re-lit it. They both knew that G-Fly got some kind of psychic powers that he's in-tuned with, and it always make the hairs stand up on their backs when G-Fly make's predictions.

* * * *

It was later on that day and Julian took his bride to be "Tracy," to the movie's to see the new controversial flick "Colors," starring Sean Penn. The movie was over and they were sitting next door to the theater at the Pizza Hut enjoying a medium Meat Lovers special. "So tell me, what did your brothers say when you told them that you where going legit?" Tracy asked Julian as she sat across from him at the table looking him in his eyes.

Julian looked up and said, "Well, G-Fly didn't like it at all! He kind of took it hard and started trippin and shit. It got so tensed that we started tussling a little and then, Ty broke it up and told G-Fly that he got to respect my decision. G-Fly was kind of stubborn but realized that it was nothing that he could do but respect it, and he apologized and gave us his blessings." Julian put a little extra on it so Tracy wouldn't feel like she was responsible for G-Fly's ill feelings.

Tracy smiled and kissed the back of Julian's hand and said, "You make me so happy baby, and I'm madly in love with you."

"I love you to pretty eyes." Tracy blushed as Julian lend over and gave her a passionate kiss on the lips.

"Honey me and the baby's horny! Let go home so we can have sex." Tracy said with a seductive smile.

"Waitress, can we get the rest of this pizza put in a box to go!" Julian asked with a lustful smile in his eyes.

"Sure sir, the waitress said as she took the pizza and put it in a box to go. Julian threw a fifty dollar bill on the table for the tip as him and his pregnant fiancée walked out hand and hand.

Julian stopped at the store to pick up some item that Tracy and the baby was craving Tracy was sitting in the car listening to Guy, 'You can have a piece of my love', and singing along to herself when she notice two niggas go stand by the pay phone and another was just sitting in the car, as it ran idled in the parking lot facing the exist to the street.

One of the nigga had on a base ball cap pulled down low with sun glasses, and the other one was standing next to him looking paranoid.

Julian was in his new 560 Sec Benz with Daton wire rims on it, so Tracy automatically thought that it was a jack move. So she grabbed her purse and grabbed her 3.80 out and seen Julian walking out unaware of the two guys standing by the phone. One of the guys pulled his hoody over his head as Tracy was opening the door to get out of the Benz, then she seen the two guys pull out guns.

Julian seen Tracy jumping out of the Benz yelling and he went for his gun and started to turn around when the two men started unloading their guns into Julian's body.

Julian fell to the ground and Tracy started bussing at the two shooters. She hit the first one in the chest with four shots dropping him dead. Then turned her gun on the other shooter and her first bullet hit him in his arm as he turned his 45 automatic on her, and shot her once in the chest and twice in the stomach.

Tracy fell to the ground holding her stomach and elevated her arm up and shot the shooter in the face. The bullet skinned his cheek and he shot two more shots at Tracy hitting her in the shoulder and lower chest. Tracy laid on the ground staring at Julian and Julian laid next to her with his eyes opened twisted in a puddle of blood. A tear rolled down her pretty face as her lifeless breath left her body.

"Come on Cuzz, let roll! The driver of the car yelled out!"

"We got to get Ant Cuzz!"

Man, Ant's dead nigga let's roll….

And the two niggas jumped in the car and sped-off burning rubber.

Chapter 2
Am I My Brother Keeper?

G-Fly was in the back of a Dodge van with big Frank, who was Hector's trusted bodyguard.

"See that's the apartment over their." Big Frank pointed to the apartment where the informant was being held. "There has to be two undercover cops with him, we got to get to him tonight cause he goes to the Grand Jury tomorrow morning," Big Frank said.

"Damn, that don't give us no time then huh?" G-Fly said as Big Frank shook his head no!

"O'kay, what did you bring me?"

Big Frank smiled and unzipped a big leather bag full of guns, flash bombs, and grenades. OOOwow, shit you got grenades too? I always wanted to see what this can do! Big Frank smiled. "O'kay, G-Fly put on his gloves and grabbed two 45 automatics that had silencer on them, two extra clips, a machine gun that had straps that you could carry on your shoulder like a purse. Then he put on a bullet proof vest, and pulled his hat down low over his eyes and put on his black leather jacket and looked at Big Frank and said, "park down the street by that truck, I'll meet you down there when I'm finish."

"Where you going? You should wait and watch first!" Big Frank said as he looked at G-Fly for understanding.

"Wait for what? We ain't got no time to wait, if we wait, then it might be more police here in the morning to escort him, then we'll be fucked. So either I got to move now, or Juan's life might be over in the morning, you understand?"

Big Frank just nodded as he watched G-Fly exit the van, and he thought to himself, 'that's one hot headed kid...!'

Big Frank knew that it was an impossible mission, and he respected G-Fly for having the heart to try it. Big Frank wanted to go with G-Fly, but he had orders to stay out of sight, because if anyone saw a Mexican around during this move, then Juan ass would be cooked to say the lease.

Big Frank put back-on his afro wig and drove the van down the block and parked.

G-Fly knew that the odds were against him, but he had two things in his favor, heart, and the element of surprise and that alone have won wars for years.

G-Fly crept to the window and seen a fat white cop sitting at the kitchen table playing cards. Another one was sitting on the couch watching TV. Then he seen a Mexican man come from the back room and sat on the love seat across from the blond hair white cop.

G-Fly walked over to the door and pulled out two of his 45 automatics and took the safety off. "If I must die tonight, then let it be as a gangsta," he said to himself as he kicked in the door where the door knob and lock was and the door swung open with ease as G-Fly ran into the apartment bussin' both his guns like a crazy gangsta'.

His first shot hit the big fat white cop who was playing cards at the kitchen table, and the 45 slugs blow his brains all over the back wall as G-Fly shot him two more times and the blast knocked his body out of the chair. The other cop was in shock as he seen G-Fly turn his guns toward him, and he put his arms up across his face trying to block the bullets and the first shot went through his hand blowing it clean off, another bullet entered his chest and face killing him. His blond hair was bloody red as he slump over the couch.

G-Fly looked over at the informant who G-Fly had scared the shit out of, his right paints leg was wet from pissing on him self.

Then G-Fly smiled and raised his guns as the Mexican tried to speak, but was cut off from the flash of the 45 automatic as the slugs entered his body slinging him to the floor. G-Fly ran over and shot the informant a second time to make sure he was dead, and then he rushed into the bedroom to make sure nobody else was around.

G-Fly reloaded his 45 and walked out the apartment, as he was leaving an old white lady around 77 years old open her door and peeped out. G-Fly aimed his gun at her, as she slammed her door shut and locked it. G-Fly just laughed as he jogged down the street to the van.

Big Frank saw him coming so he started up the van but G-Fly ran pass the van and turned the corner so nobody would see him jump into the van.

Big Frank swooped around the corner and pick-up G-Fly. G-Fly jumped into the van and said, "Let's get the hell out of here!"

"Did you get him?" Big Frank asked curiously as if he already knew the answer.

"Yep, and this place is going to be swarming with police cars in a minute, so I would advise you to get us the hell up out of here amigo!"

"Don't worry my friend I got you!" Big Frank said, holding back his excitement.

Five minutes later Big Frank pulled into a garage. Him and G-Fly went inside the house and Big Frank said you're safe now my friend. I'll call Hector, grab you some clothes from the closet and

take a shower so you can clean the gun powder
residue off yourself.

"Gracies," G-Fly said as he went to take a
shower.

G-Fly took a shower and got dress in a Nike
sweat suit and Nike shoes that was in the closet. The
shoes were a size and a half too big, but it didn't
matter because G-Fly had an extra set of clothes in his
Benz that he would change into when he got there.

G-Fly walked out of the bedroom and was
greeted by Hector.

"Comma esta my brother!"

"Comma esta Hector!" They both smiled and
embraced, each-other.

"How did it go my friend?"

"It went well Hector, it was two cops with him
though, but I took care of them too."

"I told you Frank, they are just like our brother
Game! Tell me, what happened my friend," Hector
asked?

"Well, I looked through the window and seen
how many people was there and where they were at,
and I just kicked in the door and started shooting. I
killed both of the cops first, then I shot the Mexican
with the wavy hair and tattoo on his neck in the head
and blow his muthafucken brains out."

Hector knew by the brief description that G-Fly
got Tony. "Gracies my brother, Juan owes you his
life, and we all are very grateful for your loyalty and
devotion to us. If ever you need us for anything then
just call. We are bounded for life."

"Thank you Hector, it was a honor to be able to
assist you, and your family."

Hector gave G-Fly a strong embrace and said, "Frank will take you back to your car and he will dispose of the guns and your clothes for you."

"No disrespect to you or Big Frank, but I was always taught to dispose of my own dirt!"

"No problem my friend....just be careful on your drive home," Hector said.

"I will my friend."

Big Frank dropped G-Fly off at his car and G-Fly went to get rid of his clothes that he used for the hit, then went to San Diego Beach and throw the guns in the ocean. He looked up at all of the stars in the sky and said, "Thanks for having my back Game!" Then he blasted a joint as he watched the waves for a minute, then jumped back in his car and headed back home.

* * * *

Ty was kicking back at the mansion watching the "Terminator," on his big screen TV when the phone rung. He paused the movie to answer the phone and said, "Yo, what's good?"

"Ty?"

Ty recognized Princess voice and said; "Hey beautiful... what's poppen?"

"I just got a call from Wheels, who said that one of his worker called him and said that he seen Julian's Benz at the liquor store on Vernon yellow-taped-off and policemen were all over it!"

Ty jumped up and said, "Slow down Princess, what did you say?"

"They hit Julian Ty! Ty heart dropped as Princess said, "I called around and they took him to King Medical Hospital."

"O'kay, I'm on my way....I'll meet you there!" Ty said as he hung up the phone and put his tennis shoes back on, and ran into the kitchen where Lady-G was fixing herself some butter-pecan ice cream and walnut chocolate chip cookies.

"Lady-G, Lady-G!"

"What boy," Lady-G said, and noticed a bad look on Ty's face as he ran up to her.

"Someone just hit Julian," Ty muttered.

"What?"

"Princess just called me and said that his car was taped off on Vernon at the liquor store, and policemen were all over it. She found out that they took him to King Medical Hospital."

"What about Tracy?"

"I don't know, but we need to go."

"O'kay, run and grab my coat and tennis shoes out of the bedroom upstairs, and don't forget my purse," Lady-G hollered as Ty ran upstairs to her bedroom.

"Oh my God." Lady-G said as she walked her pregnant self to the front-door holding her big stomach. Ty met her at the front-door and helped her put on her tennis shoes and coat as they rushed out. Ty held the car door opened for Lady-G to get in and then he jump in on the driver side of his mustang 5.0 and sped-off to the hospital.

They made it to the hospital in record time. Princess and Tish pulled up as Ty and Lady-G was getting out of the car. Princess pulled her new Vett in front of Ty's 5.0 as she and Little Tish jumped out and ran up to Ty and Lady-G.

They all started walking toward the entrance of the hospital as Princess began explaining to them how she got the word about Julian getting hit. They entered the main lobby of the hospital and the place was packed. They walked to the front desk and Ty said, "Excuse me Miss," to the nurse who was behind the desk.

"Yes, can I help you?"

"Do you have a Julian Johnson admitted here?"

Ty used Julian's alias that Julian uses on his driver license.

"Yes we do, are you his family?"

"Yes, he's my brother and this is our sister's"

"I think you better speak to his doctor." She said, as she turned to walk away.

"What about Tracy Martin?" Lady-G shouted out as the person behind the desk, held up her hand and walk away to grab the doctor.

"Rude Bitch," Lady-G said, as she looked over at Princess and Little Tish while they were shaking their heads in agreement.

A young white doctor walked up to Ty and said, "Pardon me sir, the nurse tells me that you're here for Mr. Julian Johnson."

"Yes doctor! He's my brother and this is our sister's."

The doctor looked over at Princess and Little Tish, and Ty said, "How is he?"

"Well I'm sorry to say he's not doing good!"

"Oh my God!" Lady-G uttered; as Princess put her arm around her to prevent her from passing out.

"What happened doctor," Ty asked?

"Apparently your brother was a victim of a fatal shooting."

"How fatal?"

"Well, he got shot seven times with a high caliber gun!"

"Oh Shit!" Little Tish screamed as she grabbed her mouth.

"We got him in surgery right now and I won't know more until later..!" Ty shook his head in a daze!

"What about Tracy Martin," Lady-G asked?

The doctor shook his head and said, "His lady friend didn't make it."

"And the baby," Lady-G said, holding back the tears from streaming down her face.

"From what I understand the lady that was with him; got shot in the stomach numerous times and the baby died with her, I'm sorry!"

Princess caught Lady-G in her arms just in time before she hit the floor, "Oh my God she fainted!"

Ty rushed over and grabbed Lady-G and helped hold her up, and as he was supporting her in his arms from hitting the floor he looked down and said, "She's peeing on herself."

"Oh shit her water broke!" The doctor yelled, "nurse, I need a gurney this minute; code red."

Within seconds, doctors and nurses were running in from all direction and placed Lady-G on a gurney and rushed her into emergency.

"I'll go with her you guys check on Julian and find G-Fly!" Princess said.

Ty Looked over at Little Tish as tears rolled down her cheeks. Ty put his arm around Little Tish, and gave her a hug and said, "We got to go call G-Fly," and they both started walking fast to find a pay phone.

* * * *

G-Fly arrived back home at the mansion at 1:15 a.m. and was surprised to see that nobody was home.

He went up stairs and jumped in the shower and when he was done he step out of the shower, and saw that his pager was vibrating on the night stand. He picked it up and seen an unfamiliar number with the code 718 after the number. His eyes got big because this was the emergency code for trouble that only him, Ty, Julian and Lady-G knew. The seven represented the "G" in the alphabet, and the eighteen represent the "R", short for "G-Red." G-Fly immediately picked up the phone and dialed the number back.

"Talk to me!" G-Fly said as Ty answered the phone on the other end.

"Fly, they hit Julian and killed Tracy." Ty said as he heard silence from the other end of the line. "G-Fly, did you hear me?"

"Yeah, I heard you....where are you?"

"I'm at King Hospital, Julian's in surgery now and they don't know if he's gonna' make it. Also, Lady-G's here with me and she just went into labor."

"Alright, I'm on my way." G-Fly said as he hung up the phone, got dress and ran out the door.

Twenty minutes later G-Fly arrived at the hospital, and as he walked into the entrance he seen two homicide police detective walk away from Ty and Little Tish as they were standing by the vending machines. G-Fly walked up to Ty and Little Tish, and Little Tish grabbed him and gave him a tight hug as he looked into her tear stained red eyes and knew that it was bad.

"They killed Tracy and the baby, and Julian is fighting for his life. The police said, that they believe that Julian was ambushed by three black men, and a witness told them that Tracy jumped out of the car and shot two of his attackers and killed one before the other one shot her. She was shot in the chest and stomach numerous times, Julian was shot seven times and one bullet pierced his spin. They got a specialist with him now trying to reconstruct his vertebrate. He might not be able to walk if he makes it!" Ty explained as his eyes watered-up from his anger.

Princess walked up and gave G-Fly a strong hug and said, "Congratulation daddy you're the proud father of a seven pound four ounce healthy baby boy." Everyone smiled and gave him a hug.

"Is she alright?" G-Fly asked Princess.

"Yes, she'll be fine! I think the hurt from hearing about Julian, Tracy and the baby caused her to have a premature birth. But the doctor said that the baby's healthy and strong. He must have known that it was time for him to come out, so he made his exist!" Princess said, as she smiled and rubbed G-Fly back.

"Excuse me Sir;" the young doctor said as he walked up to them all standing together in a group. Everyone looked up at the doctor nervously to hear what he was about to say. "I got good news; Julian made it out of surgery fine and is in stable condition."

"That's a blessing, what about his spine," Ty asked?

"Well, from what Dr. Yang reported to me, it wasn't that serious, just a small graze that barely chip the vertebrate. Dr. Yang made some small repairs but for the most part, he should recover well and have no problem walking!"

"What a relief," said Ty, as everyone smiled and began hugging each other!

"Can we see him?"

"Well, he's unconscious right now but we've taken him up-stairs to a private recovery room, his excellent medical insurance policy provides for special accommodations. You can wait in the private waiting room that is connected to his recovery room.

"Thank you Doc!" Ty said, as they shook hands.

"You guys go up and I'll meet you. I want to go see Lady-G first and let her know the good news." G-Fly said as Ty shook his head and turn and walked away.

G-Fly asked one of the nurses which floor was maternity on, and what room was Lady-G in? He started walking down the hallway, and as he entered Lady-G's room she was holding a tiny bundle in her arms. Lady-G smiled at G-Fly as his eyes lit-up when he seen his little seed. G-Fly lend over and kissed Lady-G on the fore-head and she said, "Say hello to your little Jr.!"

"Hey little man….I see that you finally made it!" And he laughed.

"Yea, he was in a rush too!" Lady-G said, as she chuckled.

"G-Fly bent down and kissed his new little son on the head and rubbed his silky hair with his lips. The baby opened his eyes and smiled and then went back to sleep. "I think he recognized your presence here," Lady-G said.

"How?"

"Probably all those times that you fad him!" G-Fly thought about it and then smiled as he caught on to Lady-G's joke.

"Have a seat over there in that chair so that the nurse can hand him to you." G-Fly sat down and the nurse placed his new little son in his arms.

"Wow, he's so tiny!" G-Fly said with pride in his eyes.

"That's because he decided to come a month early, He must've known that something was wrong." Lady-G said; with anger in her voice and a dazed look in her eyes.

G-Fly looked up at her and said, "Julian's in stable condition, he made it out of surgery fine; but his spine was grazed by one of the bullets entering in through his back, when they came up and shot him while he was laying on the ground, so the doctor thought it best to operate to make sure that there wasn't any permanent damage done to his spine, he's fine and the doctor said he'll be able to walk again.

"I knew he was too strong to leave us like that." Lady-G said, as she smiled and a tear rolled down her cheek.

The doctor walked in and asked, "Ms Jones; how are you feeling?"

"Well doctor I'm feeling much better but kind of sore!" Lady-G said in a joking manner.

"Yes, that's normal," the female doctor said, as she gave a little chuckled. "All of your tests came back and they look good, the baby has a strong heart beat and is in good health too. But, to be on the safe side, I'd like to run a few more tests. Besides, you and the baby can use the rest. So relax and we'll have you out of here in a few days O'kay?"

"O'kay doctor what ever is best."

"Are you the proud father?"

"Yes Maam."

"Well you should be happy; you have a beautiful and strong baby boy."

"I am very, very grateful Maam, and I appreciate your assistance.

"It was my pleasure! I'll have the nurse come and get the baby shortly so you can get some rest."

"O'kay," Lady-G said, as the doctor walked out of the room.

G-Fly stood up and gave the baby back to Lady-G then kissed them both and said, "I'ma go see Julian, I'll grab you and the baby some clothes and come back."

"O'kay, baby…!"

G-Fly paused and looked at his soulmate and she said, "I love you baby."

"I love you too beautiful!" G-Fly smiled and walked out.

* * * *

G-Fly made it up to Julian's floor and everyone was in the waiting room except Ty. Dee-Dee and Gwen had arrived and walked up and gave G-Fly a hug and a kiss on the cheek.

"Where's Ty," G-Fly asked?

"He's in the room with Julian, Room 716…!" Dee-Dee said as she pointed to the room.

G-Fly walked into Julian's room and his heart just dropped. Julian had tubes running all in him and was hook up to a respirator. G-Fly grabbed the wall to keep from falling, cause his legs became wobbly at the sight of seeing Julian laying there.

"You know what this means!" Ty said.

G-Fly looked over at Ty sitting in the corner with blood shot eyes and said, "you muthafucken right I do!"

"Listen I want around the clock security on this floor, so tell the girls to take turns and watch over Julian. They won't look so suspicious laying in the cut. How's Lady-G doing?"

"She's doing fine now."

"And the baby?"

"He's strong and health."

"Good, when can they leave?"

"In a couple of days the doctor said." G-Fly was speaking but his eyes were in a trance all the while gazing at Julian.

"How was your trip," Ty asked?

G-Fly's attention was broken off of Julian as he turned and looked at Ty and said, "You know how we get down!"

"That's right! And they both smiled at each other for the first time.

G-Fly walked over to Julian's side and gently grabbed hold of his fingers and said, "come on J. you got to fight man. We need you big bro, and we love you man. I know it hurts, but you got to be strong man, you can do it. I know you can fight!"

Then he bent down and kissed Julian on the forehead and swore that he felt Julian fingers move. He grinned and looked at Ty and said, "I'll go and tell the girls to take shifts on security watching over Julian. I need to go and grab some things at the mansion for Lady-G and the baby, and then I'll be back. When we're sure that our families are safe, then we can deal with this problem. Until then, I'll put some ears on the street to see what I can find out." Ty shook his head Ok! As G-Fly walked out of the room.

* * * *

"Yo Monster, what's up cuzz... this is Crime!"

"Listen, three of my soldiers caught that lame ass nigga Julian and laid him down."

"I don't know! They say that his bitch didn't make it, and I think that he's in critical!"

"Yea, I'll check into it for you. You know how we get down!"

"That's what I'm talking about! We should have it on lock in a month tops."

"Yea, I got you!"

"I'll keep you informed, I'm out!" Crime hung up the phone and began smiling.

Chapter 3
Loyal To the Game!

Lady-G and the baby came home two days after the incident. Princess, Little Tish, Gwen, and Dee-Dee were taking turns watching over Julian as he continued to fall in and out of consciousness. Lady-G went to see Julian before she left the hospital and her eyes couldn't hide the hurt as tears ran down her face. She knew that who ever was behind this attack, was living on borrowed time. She kissed Julian on the lips and whispered, "This is for Tracy," and she turned and walked out of his hospital room with the smell of blood in her nostril and murder on her mind.

Julian regained consciousness three days later, when he opened his eyes he saw Ty, G-Fly and his mother Erica all sitting in his hospital room. Ty glanced over and saw Julian's eyes open and said, "Oh shit, what's up my nigga....look ya'll he's awake."

Everyone jumped up and ran over to his bed, "I'll go grab the nurse," G-Fly said as he ran out.

"Just relax honey, don't try to get up yet. You had an accident and ..." Erica words were cut off by Ty, "Listen my nigga, some fools got at you and shot you up. You were unconscious for three days and you just woke up"

Julian looked from Ty to his mother then back at Ty as his thoughts try to digest all the information. G-Fly ran back in with the doctor, a nurse, and Lil Tish trailing behind them.

"Hello Mr. Johnson!" The doctor said as Erica looked surprise at the mention of the doctor addressing her son by the wrong name, and G-Fly looked at her and shook his head as if he read her thoughts. "You gave us a bit of a scare son, let me run some tests. Your vital signs are good... your heart and lungs seem to be working normal. Can you move your toes?"

Julian wiggled his toes, as every one in the room held their breath as he did what the doctor said, "That's great," Now move your fingers! Good! Can you move your right leg? O'kay now the left! Good....! Now I'm going to raise you up a bit, how does that feel?

"Painful..!"

"O'kay! Nurse I want to take him down and run a cat scan and x-rays on him." His family can wait here in his room and we'll keep you posted."

"O'kay doctor.... Love you baby! Julian mom said as everyone else waved and smiled. The nurse called in two orderlies and they rolled Julian in his bed down to x-ray.

* * * *

After Julian got thoroughly checked out, Ty and G-Fly went into is hospital room and told him everything that occurred as well as Tracy and the baby's death. Julian's eyes got watery and red, but no tears dripped. He was devastated by the news and you could tell that his heart turned cold with hatred.

"Who was it," Julian asked?

"We don't know and we don't trust this room to be elaborating on certain issues, so pull yourself together so we can take you home. We hired a nurse specialist to take care of you at home, but we need the doctor's permission to release you.

The hospital specialist is coming today to check and see if your spin is ok, then we might be able to take you home. Lady-G and the girls is making the needed funeral arrangements for the Tracy and baby to be buried together. Don't worry about anything; you just need to get yourself back together for us....it's work to be done." Ty explain as him and G-Fly stood over Julian's bed.

"Get you some rest my nigga ....we got around the clock security here for you. So if you see the girls running in and out then you know what it is. We'll be back later to check on you," G-Fly said.

Just then G-Fly's pager went off. He looked at the number and seen the code. He tapped Julian on the leg as him and Ty left out.

G-Fly looked over at Ty as they left Julian's room and said, "This is Hector's code."

Ty's eyes got big as G-Fly picked up his cell phone and called Hector back on his number.

"What's good amigo!" G-Fly said as the other person answered the phone,

"Hey Big Frank! Yea, I'm doing good!"

"O'yeah!"

"O'Kay, where you at?"

"Yea, I know the place. Give me 5 to 10 minutes! Yea....O'kay,later." (click)

G-Fly turned and looked at Ty and said, "Hector sent us a present, Big Frank is waiting for us at the gas station on Slauson."

"Let go then," Ty said. As they waved at Dee-Dee and left.

* * * *

When they arrived at the gas station they saw Big Frank in a new Porch. They pulled up on side of him and Big Frank started up his car and said, "Follow me," as he pulled off and G-Fly and Ty followed him. He pulled up on a side street and parked, and then they all got out and embraced one another.

"Ty, Fly....what's happening my brothers!"

Ty and G-Fly smiled at the way Big Frank addressed them with more respect and appreciation. Ty knew that G-Fly must've really put in some major work to gain this kind of acceptance.

"What's up Big Frank.... Look at you loosing weight. I might have to start calling you Little Frank in a minute."

"Don't laugh" Big Frank said, "the wify got me on a diet, I got to stay healthy!"

"That's Right," Ty said.

"So what's up Big Boy is everything good?" G-Fly said with a curious look on his face.

"Yes my friend, everything is fine." Hector sent you a present to show his appreciation on your assistance."

"Man that's not necessary, we're family we're suppose to watch each other back." G-Fly said firmly.

"No my friend, you sacrificed your life for our family and we are forever grateful." Big Frank said as Ty glanced over at G-Fly and smiled. G-Fly never told Ty the extent of what he did, because too much had occurred and it wasn't something to brag about. Ty knew that G-Fly handled his business and came back unharmed and that's all that mattered.

"Listen my brothers, it's getting real hot because of the two cops that died, so we have to move slower now. We don't want to move back and forth so much. So Hector sent you guys a thousand kilos, and Big Frank nodded toward the big u-haul truck that was parked across the street.

"You park a thousand birds on the street like this? Ty asked with a surprise look on is face!

"Of course my friend, but we put security on it."

G-Fly and Ty looked toward the end of the block and saw a car at both ends with Mexicans sitting in them.

Big Frank laughed and said, "Smart, not crazy!" And Ty and G-Fly started laughing too.

"Now, 200 kilos is a present from Hector he sent his respect. The other 800 kilos you pay us after you finish and we'll bring you guys 1000 kilos at a time so we won't have to run back and forth so much. O'kay?"

"O'kay my friend we can handle that, but let us go grab some money and give it to you, so you can take back and we'll give you the rest when we finish." G-Fly said, as Ty shook his head yes in agreement.

"O'kay my friend, but you don't have to pay us now, we trust you!"

"No we insist!" Ty said.

"O'kay."

"Listen Big Frank, go get a hotel room and page us when you get it, and we'll go put this up and grab some money so you can take back with you, O'kay!"

"O'kay my friend, I'll call you in 30 minutes also, I put 200 pounds of that good weed in there for you; from me!" Big Frank said as he smiled and held his arms out for a hug. They hugged and Big Frank handed them the keys and said, "Drive safe my friend."

"You know I will." G-Fly said as he looked at Ty and said, "You follow me, we'll take it to the South Pasadena spot."

"O'kay," Ty said as he jumped in his new 300ZX and watched as G-Fly pulled-away in the big u-haul.

After unloading the dope at the safe house, G-Fly and Ty went to another one of their safe house and grabbed five million that they had stashed there and took it to Big Frank to cover the majority of what they owed. Now all they owed was three million and that wasn't nothing but a weeks worth of work.

* * * *

"Hi baby!" Lady-G said as she walked up to G-Fly with the baby in her arms and gave him a passionate kiss.

G-Fly smiled and said, "Mmmm... that was good," and Lady-G giggled as she gave him another kiss then G-Fly kissed his son and said, "Hey little G, how's my little gangsta' doing?"

"He is not going to be no gangsta', he's going to be a doctor, lawyer, or politician!"

"Lawyers and politicians are gangsters too! That's why the world is so fucked up now." G-Fly said as he laughed and Lady-G giggled and shook her head in disbelief.

"Baby, all of the funeral arrangements have been made, and I've converted the downstairs bedroom for Julian and brought some medical equipment that he will need. Robin our hired nurse took me shopping and we pick out everything that she will need to take care of him. She going to talk to Dr. Moore and see if she can convince him to release Julian as early as tomorrow. She'll mention to him that we're willing to pay for his house calls, and he should really like that, considering that would mean more money for him in his pocket if he agrees to it.

"Great, I see that you've been on your job!"

Of course you know that I got to hold my family down. Oh, and by-the-way, I hired a nanny to move in and help us with the baby and the housework."

"Who is she," G-Fly asked?

"She's an older lady who was married to one of Games workers back in the day. Her husband, Mark use to drive for Game about two years ago. Mark died of a heart attack and Game paid for his funeral, sent his daughter to college, and blessed Cindy with a couple of dollars to get her on her feet. Anyway, we've always been good friends and when she found out that I was pregnant, she told me if I ever needed a baby sitter then to call her. So I thought that it would be nice to have a nanny for the baby and she came to mind. She's a sweet person and I know everyone will love her." Lady-G said with a spoil puppy look on her face.

"Don't be looking at me like that…. She better be nice, clean, can cook and knows how to mind her own business or she's out of here!"

Lady-G smiled, "she's nice and from the streets, so she knows her place. Watch you'll see!"

"Watch you'll see," G-Fly repeated sarcastically; "You better hope Ty and Julian like the old bitch or they're going to be mad at you!"

"They will, you'll see!"

The phone rung and G-Fly answered it, "What's good?"

"What's up Fly! I'm at the hospital with Princess and Little Tish, they're releasing J so we'll be home in about 30 minutes," Ty said.

"Good, we'll be expecting you."

"In a minute."

"Later!"

As G-Fly hung up the phone he turned around and said, "The hospital is releasing Julian and they'll be here in 30 minutes.

The intercom buzzer rung to the outside gate, G-Fly took a look at the intercom monitor and saw a taxi waiting to be let in. Lady-G said, "Oh, that's Cindy....right on time," as she push the button to open the front cast-iron gate. "Now you be nice," she said, to G-Fly.

G-Fly followed Lady-G on the porch as the taxi pulled up. A short older dark skin heavy set lady got out of the taxi, and walked up and gave Lady-G a hug and a kiss on the cheek, then she look at the baby and smiled and kissed him on his little hand. G-Fly this is Cindy.... Cindy, this is my prince charming G-Fly."

"Please to meet you sir, I heard a lot of wonderful things about you."

"Like wise." G-Fly said as he looked over at Lady-G and smiled.

"Let me grab your bags,... Lady-G tells me that you're an excellent cook, Cindy."

"Yes, I've been told that!"

"Well I look forward to finding out."

G-Fly walked over to the taxi cab driver and handed him a hundred dollar bill and said, "Keep the change."

"Thank you sir," the taxi driver said as he smiled and jump back into his cab and drove-off.

G-Fly took Cindy bags to her new room, then washed is hands and grabbed his son little G and went to watch the news while Lady-G showed Cindy around.

* * * *

Ty arrived with Princess and Little Tish at the mansion just when the ambulance pulled up in the driveway. The Medical Tech's opened the back doors and lifted Julian out and rolled him into the mansion on a stretcher.

When he was inside they carried him into his new bedroom were he looked around and saw how they had fixed everything up for his comfort. The room was filled with hospital equipment, a high rise king-size medical bed, with a pulley to hold onto when he sat up in bed. An exercise treadmill when he started walking again slowly. Also, a automatic remote control wheel-chair that reclined and was equipped with a four-wheel drive turning capacity control, to move about the mansion on his own power, without depending on anyone's help. The ladies had also furnished Julian bedroom with a surround-sound entertainment center fully equipped.

Dee-Dee and Gwen arrived thirty minutes later, and G-Fly called a meeting. They all sat down at the black marble round-table as Julian was pushed at the front end in his wheel chair.

Everyone had a serious look on their face because they knew what was coming next.

G-Fly started off and said, "I don't have to tell you what's going down or the extent of this situation because you already know. But for the sake of the naïve, let me clarify. We are in the middle of a drug war. These gangsters want our territory, our money, and our lives. And they will not stop coming until they get it! Now what do we do about it? Do we tuck our tails between our ass and run, or kill any and all that opposes us? Now they've shed first blood, so it's on in a major way now.

You all got two choices now, you can walk away now and take your wealth and materialistic gain and live problem free in another state or country,(and he looked straight at Julian) or you can stay down with your family and go to war for what we inherited, and is rightfully ours. It's your choice! If you want to leave and walk away from this shit, then just get up now and walk out... nobody will try to stop you or do anything to you for choosing to leave, it's totally your decision and we will respect it. Just get up and walk out now!"

G-Fly looked around the room and everyone was still seated. Then each person took a glance around the table at each other, and then they turned and looked over at Julian who was looking at his loyal soldiers and then he turned his eyes away and staring at the table with his head held down. G-Fly said, "Well I guess that it's us against the muthafucken world then!" And everyone smiled, as G-Fly continued; "Check it out, these muthafuckas killed my sister... killed my god-son, and tried to kill my brother! Now I don't know what's on your mind, but my mind is inflicted with the thought of revenge and murder. Now I want to know who's responsible for this hit, and I want him dead and everyone who's down with him dead! Tomorrow we will bury our sister and our god-son, after that, we will paint the streets of L.A. red with blood!"

After that everyone who was seated around the table started clapping and shouting "yes-yes" expressing their approval.

"Now listen Ty said, I want to starve the streets of L.A. so we can see our enemies better. I want to know who else is moving big weight out here, so we can get a pin point on who's who and what they got going on. Once we see who's doing what, then we move in for the kill. When our workers start loosing money then they're going to either ride with us or fall with them. I want ya'll in rental cars only, until we find out who's our primary enemies. Then after we smash them; we can go back to balling. Be careful out there and shot first then ask questions! Does everyone understand…. any questions?"

"Yes, I have a question? So you don't want us to give Wheels his work this week, so he can hold down his spots." Dee-Dee asked?

"Nope, don't give him shit!" Ty said.

"What about Paper and our outer city clients." Princess asked?

"Fuck Paper and them, they might be the ones who are out to get us." G-Fly strongly reemphasized!

"Nobody get's shit, it's a drought! I don't care if a nigga wants to pay you 25g's for a key; you better not sell him shit! We run this city and whoever wants it is going to have to kill us all to get it….we're officially at war; and I expect to see some bodies falling! Do you ladies understand?"

"Yes"

"Yes daddy"

"I'm with it to the fullest," Little Tish muttered underneath her voice.

"Me too," Gwen said as she gave Little Tish high five.

"I know you bitches was crazy when I first met you!" G-Fly said as everyone laughed and Julian grabbed his side as to not feel the pain because he couldn't hold back his laughter.

"Do you want to say something Julian," Ty asked?

"I just want to say thank you all and I love you all to death!"

"Fuck all that emotional shit… that's what we do, we ride for each other and the cause. We're muthafucken gangsters." Everyone started shouting and gave their approval.

"This muthafucken meeting is adjourned! Cock your guns and let's ride."

Yea, let's get the hell up out of here," and everyone clapped and embraced each other with support and a farewell kiss good-bye.

Chapter 4
In The Name Of War!

It was the day of the funeral and everyone was still in mourning. Julian was silent all the way through the ceremony as tears ran from underneath his dark glasses. Little Tish was pushing him around in his wheel chair and couldn't hold back her tears as she stared at the baby coffin that sat next to Tracy closed casket. Ty had to relieve Little Tish as he stood over Julian and said, "Be strong my nigga, vengeance is ours!" Julian looked up at Ty as tears ran down his face and shook his head 'O'kay!

Big Max and his security crew was posted every where on guard. Only the immediate family and the ladies that worked for the escort service was welcome and privileged to attend the funeral. Tracy didn't have no family other then the one that Julian gave her, so it was a small attendance.

Lady-G had white doves release from a cage at the end of the funeral and it made a lot of people smile at the thought of finally being free.

The gathering was held at the night club that Diamond and Treasure, (two of the ladies that worked for the escort service) started with the youngster as a silent partner. The club was closed to the public, so that the family members could gather in peace.

After the gathering every one went their separate ways and it seemed like their sadness only agitated the anger that was burning inside all of them.

The following day Julian was laying in his bed caught-up in his sorrow and distracted in memories of Tracy and what could have been their life together. Just then G-Fly walked in holding his baby-boy.

"What's up my nigga," Julian just nodded his head.

"Are you going to lay in bed all day and drown in your own sorrow, or are you going to get your ass out of that bed so we can roll?"

"Nigga, I can't walk!"

"That's bullshit, I never heard you say that you couldn't do something. All that weak ass shit got to go!"

"Man fuck you, you don't know what it feels like to get shot seven times and the doctor tells you that your spine was damage and it's a possibility that you might not walk again!" Julian anger was heating up as he tried to argue his defense.

"Ha, ha, ha! Nigga your pathetic! You're gonna believe everything that a cracker tells you? You know that white people been lying to us all of our life. He's getting paid to lie to you; cause every time he needs some pocket money he comes here to see you and tells you just to lay down and relax so he can come back in a couple of more days and get another thousand dollars for doing nothing! Shit he wishes that he can come and see you a hundred times a week so he can really stack-up a grip."

Julian turned his head to the side so that he wouldn't have to look at G-Fly in his eyes.

"Nigga you need a reality check cause this shit ain't GP."

"Here…!" G-Fly gave Julian the baby to hold.

"What you want me to do with him?"

"Since both of ya'll like to be pampered, I thought that ya'll should get together and talk about who's going to be the biggest baby around here." G-Fly said laughing as he walked away.

"Wait… G-Fly! Come on man, I can't take care of no baby!"

"Why not, that's your god son! But you never know, he's very strong….jumped right out of his momma's pussy a month early when he heard about your accident. So he might have to take care of your weak ass. Ha, ha, ha!

"G-Fly, G-Fly this shit ain't funny nigga!" Just then the baby started crying and Julian hollered Lady-G…., Cindy; someone help!"

Lady-G was by Julian's bedroom door when G-Fly walked out and she remarked, "you're scandalous!" Then she heard Julian calling her name again and she started giggling.

"He needed a reality check, so I told little G to give him one," and they both started laughing.

Cindy was in the kitchen when she heard Julian calling her so she was on her way to see what was wrong with him when G-Fly stopped her and said, "he's alright, little G is just giving him a small reality check. Let the babies be together for a while."

"Yes sir Mr. Fly," and she started giggling and walked back into the kitchen.

Julian saw the baby's bottle that G-Fly left on the dresser next to his bed and he reached over and grabbed it and gave it to the baby. Little G stopped crying and started drinking his milk.

"Don't worry little man, uncle J got you! You're going to have it all, anything you want! And you're going to the best college and you will be someone successful and rich, a player like your uncles!" Julian smiled at little G as he held him in his arms and then he kissed him on his little head.

Lady-G was outside Julian's door listening to Julian kick game to little G and she smiled as she enjoyed the strong emotional bond that he was building with little G.

* * * *

G-Fly and Ty was at one of their stash spots counting the money that Princess and the girl brought them from the last pick-up and the previous work that was sold.

"I got $730,000 dollars over here," Ty said.

"I got $680,000 dollars over here plus, Princess and them still got 30 birds put up," G-Fly said.

"That's $1,410,000 thousand dollars and we still got 50 birds left over from the last batch. So we did pretty good!" Ty said with a smile, just then his pager went off. He looked at the number and said, "It's Killa."

"Didn't you already tell him that he got to go through the girls for work now?" G-Fly asked.

"Yea, he already knows that I don't touch no work like that!"

"Maybe he's desperate!" G-Fly said looking at Ty suspicious.

"Hell naw nigga, this is family....he'll never jump bitch on us." Ty said; defending his cousin integrity cause he knew that G-Fly was assuming that desperate niggas set people up when they fall weak. Ty picked up his cell phone and called Killa's number.

"Yo what's up cousin?" Killa said when he answered the phone on the first ring.

"Problems, struggle, questions, you know the issues." Ty said.

"Yea, I know my nigga, and I was calling because I ran across your needle in a haystack and you need to come and holla"

"Yea?"

"Where are you at?" Ty asked.

"I'm at the new condominium in west LA off of Crenshaw, you know the spot!"

"Yea, me and G-Fly's on our way!" Ty said as he hung up and looked at G-Fly and said, "Killa found that nigga who shot Julian."

"No shit...!" G-Fly's eyes got big as he and Ty started putting the money away and grabbing their guns and bullet proof vests, then they left out on a mission.

* * * *

"Yo Charlie, pull up slow cuzz....right here!" Gangsta said, as he squatted down in the back seat of the car.

"Call him over to the car! Let him know that you got a hundred that you want to spend." Gangsta whispered softly.

"What would you give me for a hundred," the old base head Charlie said as he pulled up on the spot where Tim-Tim, Dre and Fat Rob be serving at on one of Wheels dope street's.

"Pull over there and park and get out of the car." Tim-Tim said as he looked at the old man suspiciously and grabbed the butt of his 9mm.

"He wants me to pull over and park and get out of the car," the old man said."

"Fuck that shit," Gangsta said, as he lifted up from the back seat and started shooting his 12 gage sawed-off shotgun. YG Crip was bent down in the back seat too, and when he seen his homeboy Gangsta start bussin', he jumped up with his Mac 10 and started bussin' at Dre who was serving another smoker at the other end of the street.

Tim-Tim saw a head bobbing up from the back seat of the Chrysler New Yorker and Tim-Tim said, "It's a hit" and jumped behind a parked car right before the 12 gage shotgun went off and pierced the cement wall full of buck shots.

Dre heard the gun shot of the 12 gage and turned and looked just as YG Crip started bussin' his Mac 10 at him. Dre dove on the ground as the old base head, who he was serving got lit-up as multiple bullets riddled his body. Dre crawled along-side a parked car as one of the bullets ricochet and hit his leg.

"Damn," Dre said as he heard the bullets stop and he jumped up and started bussin' his 357 magnum at the front window of the Chrysler as he seen Tim-Tim raise up from behind a park car and started unloading his 9mm into the side window.

Fat Rob was around the vacant house getting his dick sucked by a young smoker bitch as he heard all hell brake loose. He snatch his dick from the smoker mouth and stuffed it back in his pants as he ran back out front with his new 45 automatic in his hands. He saw Tim-Tim and Dre bussin' at the Chrysler so he started busting his 45 at the car too.

Gangsta said, "Drive muthafucka drive."

YG Crip was squatted down on the floor board of the car reloading his Mac 10 as he looked up and seen the old man slumped over the stirring wheel dead. "He's dead....Charlie's dead!" YG Crip hollered.

"Move his ass out the way and drive this muthafucka then." Gangsta yelled at YG Crip.

YG Crip was wrestling with Charlie's died body as Dre and Tim-Tim was reloading. Gangsta raised up and shot 3 shot from his 3.80 at Fat Rob and Fat Rob jumped behind a tree, as YG Crip finally got old man Charlie's dead body out of the way, and stomp on the gas as the Chrysler took off and bullets rattled the back window as the car turned the corner and was gone.

"Are ya'll alright cuzz?" Tim-Tim asked.

"I'm cool," Fat Rob said.

"That bitch ass muthafucka shot me in the leg cuzz!" Dre said in an angry tone.

"Look, they got old man Sam." Dre said.

"Damn, let's take him over by the railroad tracks so the spot won't get hot. Dre go see if Ms. Fay can help you. Also, call Wheels and tell him what just happen. Come on Fat Rob let's get rid of Sam's body before the nosy neighbors start circling around him, Tim-Tim said.

They threw old man Sam's body in the trunk of the car and left the dope spot.

Twenty minutes later the police drove up and down the dope street twice and when they didn't see anything they just drove off and went on about their business.

* * * *

Ty and G-Fly arrived at Killa's new condo and was greeted with a strong ghetto embrace from Ty's big cousin.

"What's up little nigga's ya'll to big now to come holla at your folks." Killa said playfully.

"Naw, Killa man....we just been up against it. Niggas is trying to slump a nigga on some scandalous gangsta shit." Ty explained.

"I feel you, I went through the same shit when I first started playing with weight....so I can imagine what ya'll going through." G-Fly shook his head and made a facial expression displaying his troubles. "But don't worry, I got your back!"

"I was at the casino by the race track and this nigga was running his mouth about pushing big weight. At first I didn't really trip until a bitch who he was trying to impress asked him what happened to his face.

He had a fresh wound on his face like it was just healing up and he said that it was a beauty mark. Then confessed that he just recently had a shoot-out and got shot in the arm and grazed in the face by a bullet."

She said that, "someone must've been really mad at him." He laughed and said, "some jealous niggas tried to rob him."

"Right then it came to me, that this must be one of the niggas who put the lick down on Julian. I was going to follow the nigga home and smoke him, but I felt that ya'll would want to handle it yourself, so I pushed up on him and told him that I'm looking for a new connect because my old Mexican connect got smoked two weeks ago.

He seemed excited to hook up, so I called him that night and brought a bird to get on his good side, and to see how he functioned. The nigga met me and was alone, and I told him that if it's good then I want five more.

He said he'll give them to me for $13,500 all day. We chopped it up briefly and come to find out he's a crip working for some niggas out of Compton, who's out here trying to set up shop. Once he found out that I was a crip too, then he seem more relaxed, and told me to get at him anytime and he got me. He goes by the name Crazy!"

"Damn my nigga, we love you for this one." G-Fly said as he gave Killa dap.

"Ya'll my little nigga's, you know that I'ma ride for you."

"Peep call this nigga up and we'll snatch his punk ass up and deal with him." Ty said as they all smiled.

"I'ma tell the nigga to meet me at the spot on 120th so we can gag him in the house, then ya'll can take him where ever and do your thang."

"Gratitude my nigga, we owe you big time," Ty said.

"Nigga we're family, you know that I got your back, and Ty and Julian too. I raised you little bad ass niggas." Killa said as they all smiled and walked out headed to the spot.

* * * *

Crazy walked into Killa spot by himself without any signs of having any dope on him. Killa had stacks of money already on the kitchen table counted out. Killa order 5 kilos but questioned weather Crazy was stupid enough to trust him and bring the dope.

"Ah cuzz my bad! I just wanted to make sure that you had that kind of money before I brung the dope in. You know it's hard to trust a nigga when you don't really know him." Crazy explained.

"I feel you cuzz....so where is the dope?" Killa asked as he gripped the butt of his 357 magnum.

"Oh don't trip my nigga, I got it in the car, let me get it." Crazy opened the front door and took out his bic cigarette lighter and flicked it twice, then did it again, and another nigga got out of the car; went to the trunk and grabbed a duffle bag, closed the trunk and walked into the house with Killa and Crazy.

"Oh ya'll got signals," Killa laughed as he shut the door and said, "go and count the money cuzz, it's all good."

As Killa was speaking Ty and G-Fly ran out of the back room with guns drawn.

"Go for it! I'll blow your muthafucken head off nigga," G-Fly said as he pointed his big 44 magnum at Crazy's head, and Ty had Crazy homeboy dead bang with his two new 9mm.

"Get on the ground nigga!" Ty ordered as they both laid down on the floor.

Killa grabbed the duffle bag and unzipped it and smiled when he seen the 5 birds.

"It's like this cuzz!" Crazy said as he looked up at Killa! G-Fly then hand cuffed both of them, then used a taser gun on them both.

"You ain't seen the worse yet nigga," Killa said as he laughed.

G-Fly searched them and took their guns off them, then took their money and jewelry and sat it on Killa's kitchen table.

"Yo, let's take these fools to the house that we got on the Westside. We can pull up in the garage and keep shit out of sight." G-Fly said.

"Cool, pull the car in the alley so we can creep these niggas out undetected."

"O'kay," G-Fly said as he pulled his black Lincoln rent-a-car around back. They gagged the two niggas and drugged them through the back door and put them in the trunk of the car.

"Ya'll need some help?" Killa asked.

"We cool now my nigga!" Ty said then look at G-Fly and said, "I'ma follow you in this niggas BMW....."

drive carefully. G-Fly nodded his head and rolled up the window and pulled out of the back yard.

* * * *

They drove to their house on the Westside and pulled the rent-a-car into the garage. They opened up the trunk of the car and pulled Crazy and his homeboy out, but not before using the taser gun on them again.

They sat them in a chair and tide them up real tight while they were still hand cuffed from behind.

G-Fly said, "You see how much information you can get out of them; I'ma go get Julian." They both smiled. "Also, set up something special so he can take his time."

"Gotcha."

G-Fly walked into the mansion and was greeted by Lady-G and the baby. He kissed them both and said, "go put on some clothes I want you and Julian to roll with me some where. Tell Cindy to watch little G while we're gone."

"O'kay daddy, is everything alright?"

"Everything is fine, now stop questioning me and do as I said."

"O'kay baby!" Lady-G said as she walked away.

G-Fly walked into Julian's room and Julian was laying down watching the basket ball game. Hey my nigga, I want you and Lady-G to roll with me some where."

"I don't feel like it." Julian mumbled.

"What," G-Fly yelled." Nigga put these sweat pants and shoes on before I drag you out of that bed and take you in your draws."

Julian looked at G-Fly and seen that he was pissed so he grabbed his pants and struggled to put them on. G-Fly help him with his tennis shoes and sweat coat, then carried him over to his wheel chair."

"Where we going,"

"Some-where special nigga why, you got something better to do?"

"You're going to make me miss the game!"

"Man fuck that game! You can watch the best parts tonight on the news." G-Fly said as he laughed.

"Fuck you nigga" Julian responded with his lips poked out.

"I'm ready," Lady-G said as G-Fly smiled at the cute out-fit and boots that she was wearing to look sexy for her man.

"Mmmm! That's my girl," G-Fly said as Lady-G blushed and they left out.

* * * *

G-Fly pulled up at the old safe-house and Julian said, "Why you come here?"

"It's your surprise party nigga." G-Fly said as he got out of the car and grabbed Julian's wheel chair and walked around to open Julian's door. The pissed-off expression on Julian face showed that he was mad, "Nigga I don't want no muthafucken party."

"Listen nigga, I'm getting tired of your whinny ass, cry baby childish ways, now either you bring your stubborn ass by choice or by force! It's your decision."

"You got that, but when I get better it's on....nigga, cause I'ma whoop your ass." Julian said as G-Fly carried him out of the car and sat him in his wheel chair.

"Yea right! You and who else? You're to soft to whoop anybodies ass, let alone mines! G-Fly said as he started laughing at the thought.

"O'kay nigga, we'll see!"

Lady-G just laughed and shook her head as they argued back and forth like little kids.

G-Fly held the front door opened as Julian hit the forward button on his remote control wheel chair and rolled in the house as Lady-G followed behind him.

"You watch and see I'ma knock your ass out again like I did when we was kids." Julian mouth was still going as G-Fly just laughed and opened up the side door to the garage. Julian rolled in as he saw Ty with two niggas tied up in two chairs. Julian looked at G-Fly, with his mouth opened in shock and said,

"What the fuck is this?"

"I told you that it was a surprise party for you." Julian rolled in front of the two niggas about 10 feet away.

"Ty did you get anything out of them," G-Fly asked?

"Yea, the one that pissed on him self got a lot to talk about but the other one Crazy here is playing tough!"

"Oh yea, well let's see how tough he is, Julian meet Crazy, Crazy meet the man that you killed his pregnant wife and unborn child. And oh yea, I forgot, the man that you tried to kill."

Crazy eyes got big as Julian stared at him like a wild lion. Julian you see that scar on the side of his face, that's the one that Tracy made right before he killed her."

G-Fly was emphasizing his words to make a point and to aggravate Julian.

"Let's see what Crazy has to say for himself?" G-Fly pulled the gag out from Crazy mouth, "Look man, I'm sorry about your girl, she wasn't suppose to get hurt. Crime and Felony put the hit out on you. They said that Monster gave the order to kill you guys on sight."

"Who's Monster, Crime and Felony," Ty asked?

"They're niggas out of Compton that's ballin out of control. They work for a kingpin named Little Creep. Little Creep wants to bring his business to LA and I guess ya'll is in his way. I didn't even know who ya'll was. The other guy that got killed was the one who was after ya'll, I was just with him at the time. They hired us just to move weight for them. I didn't know anything about a war until that night after it went down."

"Where can we find this Felony, Crime, Monster, and Little Creep?" Ty asked.

"Crime and Felony is the only one out here. Crime drives a black 500 SEL AMG Benz and Felony got a blue 600 series BMW. Monster is Little Creep lieutenant and they both stay in Compton somewhere."

"Where?"

"I don't know, I just heard Crime brag about them."

"Who do you get your work from?" G-Fly asked.

"I deal with Crime, he gives me 10 keys at a time and when I'm finished I call him and he brings me 10 more and I give him his money. I don't know where he lives at or nothing."

"Where do you meet him at?" G-Fly continued to interrogate him.

"He picks the location and I meet him there." Crazy said in a whimpering voice.

"I'll tell you what, call the nigga and tell him that you got his money and when he comes to get it, kill him and well let you both live and you can keep the money and work, this is our final proposition, take it or die?

"O'kay, I'll do that! I didn't like the way they played me against ya'll anyway."

Julian heart was burning with rage but he knew that he had to play along so he could catch the bigger fish.

"Man I'm sorry about your girl, don't worry I'll kill this nigga for you watch!" Julian just smiled and shook his head.

Lady-G was standing behind Julian and she asked herself if this nigga was really this damn stupid? His friend was still gagged and they both were tied-up, but at less you could see by the tears running down his friends face that he had sense enough to know that it wasn't going to turn out well for him and Crazy.

Crazy paged Crime from the house phone, Ty dialed the number and when Crime called back Ty held the phone to his ear.

"What's up cuzz, yea I got that!" "Where?" "O'kay" I'll be their in 30 minutes."

Ty hung up the phone. "He said for me to meet him at the Ralphs Supermarket parking lot on Slauson. I told him that I'll meet him there in 30 minutes."

"Cool that gives us just enough time." G-Fly said as he socked Crazy in the jaw and dazed him then gagged him again. Crazy started mumbling as his homeboy began crying louder.

"Julian," G-Fly said as Julian looked up at him. "He's all yours! There's some equipment over there help yourself."

Julian looked over at the table as Crazy and his homeboy did too, and setting there on the table was a big Jason knife, a hammer, a hand held axe, an electric cord, a gun and a electric saw. Julian smiled and Lady-G was about to push him over to the table when G-Fly said, "hold up baby! Watch out!" and he pull the brakes on Julian's wheel chair and said, "If you want it then you got to get up and get it yourself."

Julian looked at G-Fly and gave him a evil look then he looked up at Lady-G and she walked over and sat down on the other side of the room. Ty was standing there and when Julian looked over at him he just shrugged his shoulders and said, "It's on you now my nigga." Julian looked over at the two dudes and used his arm strength to push himself up in a standing position. He weaved back and forth for a second, and then started walking slowly like a baby to the table.

"I knew that, that nigga was faking!" G-Fly said as Lady-G and Ty smiled.

Julian made it to the table and grabbed the big Jason knife.

"Wise decision, I probably would've grabbed that one too! G-Fly said to Lady-G as they both stood there laughing.

Julian turned around with the big knife gripped tightly in his right hand and all you could see is death in his eyes as he walked slowly step by step toward Crazy. Crazy was crying and mumbling just like a baby as he started shitting in his pants begging for his life. Julian then grabbed him by his hair and pulled his neck back and began cutting his throat sawing off Crazy head.

"Oh shit, that shit is gross!" Lady-G said as she stared at the sick sight with no remorse.

After he cut through Crazy's neck as much as he could he grabbed Crazy head and broke his neck bone just like a chicken, and continue cutting the rest of the head off. Crazy's body shook uncontrollable but Julian's tight grip wouldn't let go. Blood was everywhere and Julian was covered in Crazy's blood. He looked over at Crazy's homeboy and he was shaking as if he was having a seizure and in shock. Then Julian jumped on him like a wild animal and started stabbing him multiple times in the chest, head and face.

G-Fly looked at Ty and said, "Give me your vest and guns. You clean this shit-up and me and Lady-G will go get that nigga Crime."

"O'kay my nigga, here, and be safe!"

"You too! Will bring back the G-ride and some cleaning supplies."

"Cool."

"O'kay Hannibal, see you in a minute. Julian looked up at G-Fly and then at himself covered in blood, and smiled.

* * * *

G-Fly gave Lady-G the bullet proof vest that he got from Ty, and his black boomer jacket to cover it up. She had her 3.80 automatic and G-Fly had his big 44 magnum and Ty's new 45 automatic. He also had his bullet proof vest that he wore under his black sweat shirt. They arrived at the Ralph's Supermarket parking lot and drove once through trying to get a vibe on who they where looking for. In the mist of the interrogation of Crazy, they forgot to ask him for a description. G-Fly parked in a parking spot so they could have a good view of the cars coming and going as well as already parked.

"Damn we don't know how this muthafucka looks, and we don't know if he knows how we look either!" G-Fly said to Lady-G as they both scanned the parking lot.

The parking lot was packed and cars was coming and going at random.

"Baby I got an ideal! Let's call Ty and get this nigga's pager number, then page him and see if we can catch him slipping like that." Lady-G said.

"Good idea, and G-Fly called Ty on the house phone and Ty gave them the pager number as he recalled it. G-Fly hung up and looked at Lady-G and said, "Listen, I want you to call that nigga from that pay phone over there, but stay alert we don't know if this nigga knows how we look or who he's with."

"Gotcha baby."

Lady-G kissed G-Fly and got out of the car and went over to the pay phone to call Crimes pager number.

Crime was sitting in his 88 Buick Regal rent-a-car with his homeboy Little Phil from Compton. Crime seen Lady-G walk over to the pay phone and said, "This must be my lucky day."

"What's up?" Little Phil said as he looked up from rolling a joint.

"That's that bitch Lady-G, the one who fuck with that baller nigga who we been beefing with!" Crime said.

"What do you want to do big homie," asked Little Phil?

"I'ma go mac at this bitch and see if I can crack her and if not then I'ma smoke that bitch." Crime said as Little Phil laughed and watched Crime as he got out of the car.

Lady-G hung up the phone as a light skin nigga with wavy hair and green eyes walked up to her and said, "Hey beautiful, can a brotha have a minute of your time?"

Lady-G smiled and said, "I'm married."

"I'm not trying to take you away from your man, I just want to spoil you and introduce you to the nicer thangs in life." Crime said with a player's smile as his pager went off. He reach down to look at the number, and when he looked up Lady-G was pulling out her 3.80 automatic and shot him 3 times, two shots in the chest and one in stomach. Crime tried to shield his self as he fell to the ground.

Little Phil jumped out of the car bussin' at Lady-G as she ducked in front of a park car and shot back twice in Little Phil direction. Little Phil ducked low to the ground and tried to creep across the parking lot as G-Fly caught him slippin and hit him 3 times with his big 44 magnum knocking Little Phil off his feet and he flew five feet across the parking lot. G-Fly ran over to Crime and Crime seen him coming as he laid on the ground with his 9mm gripped in his hand and he started unloading his 9mm wildly at G-Fly as G-Fly tried to dodge the bullets and shot Crime twice in the chest with the big 44 magnum, killing Crime instantly.

Lady-G had seen Crime start shooting at G-Fly as he was running up and she jumped up from in front of the parked car and started shooting at Crime 4 more times, but it was the 2 shots from G-Fly's 44 magnum that ended Crimes life, making his whole body stiffen and shake from the impact.

G-Fly just then reached down and grabbed the pager off Crimes dead body and him and Lady-G ran and jumped into the rent-a-car and sped-out of the parking lot and turned onto the main street. "Slow down baby." Lady-G hollered as he eased off the gas and started driving normal.

"Are you alright baby?" G-Fly asked as a police car drove by on the opposite side of the street headed toward Ralph's Supermarket.

"Yea, I'm fine….what about you," Lady-G asked?

"I think that he got me!" G-Fly said as he turned down a side street.

"What?" Lady-G screamed!

"I don't see any blood I think the bullet proof vest saved me."

"Pull over, let me see!"

G-Fly pulled over to the curve and Lady-G turned on the interior light and checked him for any holds or bullet wounds. She seen a bullet embedded into the stomach part of his bullet proof vest and said, "Yep, right here! But the vest stopped it. Slid over let me drive," Lady-G said, and G-Fly traded spots with her. "We got to get out of this car and get rid of it. Go to the stash spot on 53rd and 5th ave., we'll get cleaned up there and use the G-ride that's parked there. Then we'll come back and get rid of this rent-a-car. We need some gas so that we can burn this car tonight."

"O'kay baby, you know that you saved me back their." Lady-G said as she smiled over at him.

"You muthafucken right, and now you owe me your life!"

G-Fly said as he laughed holding his stomach trying to subdue the pain.

G-Fly and Lady-G both shower at the spot and change their clothes. The youngsters kept extra clothes and guns at all of their safe house, so it was convenient. They made it back to the other safe house with the bleach and cleaning supplies, and Ty had already rolled the bodies up in plastic bags and cleaned up the blood.

Julian was showered and dressed in different clothes. He was sitting on the couch smoking a joint with Ty as G-Fly walked in with Lady-G following behind him. G-Fly looked over at him and said, "You feel better now?"

Julian smiled and shook his head yes! Then he forced himself to stand up and held out his arm to G-Fly and they gave each other a hug, then he hugged Lady-G too. G-Fly said, "Your sister got rid of that nigga Crime for you. You should've seen her, she was like Foxy Brown with that heater."

"What happened?" Julian asked with excitement in his voice.

"I'll let her tell you the story as I finish cleaning up the garage with the bleach and shit. We're going to put these nigga's in the trunk of Crazy BMW and burn it, so we can kill two birds with one stone. We have to burn the rent-a-car and go get rid of them guns too."

"Cool my nigga, it's your call!" Ty said as everyone smiled at G-Fly laying down the law.

They finish disposing of everything and made it back at the mansion by 1:15a.m. They pulled up and got out of the car and G-Fly grabbed the wheel chair from the trunk and started pushing it into the entrance of the mansion, as Julian sat in the back seat of the car waiting for some assistance. G-Fly looked at him and said, "You might as well get your ass out and walk, because ain't nobody gonna baby your ass no more." And him, Ty and Lady-G laughed as they walked into the house and left the front door opened.

Julian smiled to himself then opened up the car door and pulled himself to his feet, and took slow steps into the mansion.

Chapter 5
Welcome To the Ghetto!

It was the following day and everyone was sleeping in late but Julian. Lady-G walked into the family room where Cindy had little G bathed, dressed and feed and they both was watching TV.

Lady-G said, "Hi little man, did you miss your mommy last night?" Little G's eyes were opened and staring back at his mommy.

"I cooked some breakfast for you guys, and I was waiting for ya'll to wake up before I prepared the table for you. Julian already ate."

"O'kay you fed him this morning?"

"Well yes and no." Cindy said as she let out a small giggle.

"I don't understand," Lady-G said.

"Well he walked into the dinning room and sat at the table as I was cooking, so I fixed him a big breakfast, then he went to the gym room and started working out and that's where he's at now." Cindy said as she laughed and walked away.

Lady-G picked little G up and said, "come on little man, we got to see this." And she walked into the gym room carrying little G in her arms.

Julian was on the bicycle machine as Lady-G walked in and he smiled and said, "What's up sis, I hope you slept well last night."

"I slept fine! How about you?"

"I wasn't too tired... I had a lot of energy like my body was telling me that I was strong now."

"What about your mind, did you find some sort of closure last night? You know, getting revenge and all?"

"Well, nothing can really erase the pain of loosing someone you love so much. But it made me feel powerful again, dealing with my demons like that. There's more, so I got to get ready for battle, because my family needs me at my best. I won't let them hurt nothing else that I love. You feel me?" Julian said as he slowly got off the bicycle and stood straight up with no help.

"Yea, I feel you baby, and I'm proud of you! I guess that your brother was right." Lady-G said as she smiled.

"Yea, G-Fly got a strange way of expressing it, but his love is unconditional." Julian smiled as he walked over and kiss Lady-G on the forehead and said, "You know that I love your down ass right!"

"Of course I know."

Then he kissed little G on the forehead and said, "I'm going for a swim… Ya'll want to come?"

"Naw, we'll pass on this one." Lady-G said as they looked up and seen G-Fly and Ty walking up.

"Oh shit, look Ty its Rocky!" G-Fly joked as everyone started laughing.

"What's good my nigga's?" Julian said as Ty and G-Fly gave him a ghetto embrace.

"Nothing player just glad to see you out and about," Ty said.

"Yea, I got to get right so I can ride for my niggas. We ride together and we die together….against all odds. The three Generals!" Julian said.

"You muthafucken right! Even after death were going to ride together in hell." G-Fly said as they all gave each other their ghetto handshake.

"Ya'll crazy! Come on little G you're too young to be around this." Lady-G said as she walked out of the room with little G in her arms.

"One more year little G, one more year baby boy!" G-Fly said as Lady-G was walking away and everyone laughed.

"Listen ya'll, I'ma go check up on the girls today, then stop by the other Mansions and holler at the other girls.

Cee-Cee and Egypt is ready to start their record label so I got to go and see how much money they need. I saw their proposal and they both got two hundred G's to invest, and they want us to put up four hundred thousand, but Lady-G said that they might need a little more and that we should give them a little more security, so I want to offer them a hundred and fifty thousand more to put to the side for security purposes, and if they need it, then we'll just recoup it when the business start making money. But we won't charge them nothing extra or ask for a bigger percentage. We're just making sure that they got enough to have a fair start." Ty said as he expressed his concerns.

"Sounds good to me," Julian said.

"Make it happen player and I'm glad that you said something because I still got the money from the club that I didn't deposit in the bank yet. I got to make sure that I do that today," G-Fly said.

"Your breakfast is ready," Cindy yelled into the hallway.

"That's our cue!" Ty said as he looked at Julian and said, "You coming?" As they started walking away.

"Naw, I already ate....I'm going for a swim."

"That's right my nigga get money," G-Fly said as he laughed and walked out.

＊ ＊ ＊ ＊

"Princess why them niggas trippin like that? My spots ain't had no work for a week now, and niggas is blowing up my pager like crazy. I'm loosing all kinds of paper! I got other niggas trying to come over to our block trying to sell their work."

"Listen nigga, ain't nothing moving until this war is over, so I advise you to go put on your gangsta draws and get to poppin' niggas. Either you're going to be down for the cause or fall victim to it. You feel me?" Princess said as she and Little Tish drove down the street coming from the mall.

"Yea, I feel you! But that shit is bogus." Wheels complained.

"Well you can call it what you want, but its law!"

"I hear you... I'm out" Click!
"This crazy bitch got me fucked up!" Wheels said as he went to grab a number that he had put up and paged it.

＊ ＊ ＊ ＊

"I know that this sorry muthafucka didn't just hang up in my face like that!" Princess said, as Little Tish laughed." I'll tell you, a nigga start getting a little money then gets beside himself. He ain't calling no muthafuckin' shots around here, he better hope that I don't dog his ass when it's back on."

"Girl fuck that nigga, he crum snatching anyway. We got other issues to deal with. Look at that nigga, ain't that the kind of car Ty said oh boy drives?"

"Hell ya girl, I think that that's him?" Princess said as she swooped in back of the blue BMW 600 series. As they both turned into the McDonald parking lot.

"He's going through the drive thru....go around on the other side, park over there so we can go back out the back-way." Little Tish pointed. Then she pulled out her new 45 automatic out of her purse.

Princess looked over at her and said, "Where did you get that big muthafucka at?"

Tish laughed and said, "Girl it's on out here, I need something that's gonna lay some shit down."

Princess shook her head as she took her 3.80 off safety, and said, "How you want to do this?"

Little Tish seen a lady walk by holding hands with her two daughters and said, "It's too many innocent people around here. Let's follow him and catch him at the stop light, so no innocent people will get hurt."

"O'kay, but be ready. He's getting his food now... Yep, that got to be him, a fat ugly nigga with big jewelry on."

"O'kay follow him!" Tish said.

"I got him girl, be ready and watch out for the cops, we don't need them in our business."

"Fuck the cops bitch, I'ma get this nigga! Look he missed the light, stay in the car so I can creep on the passenger side without him noticing us."

"Be careful girl." Princess yelled as Little Tish slid out of the passenger door and started creeping on the side of the blue BMW as it was stopped at the light.

Felony was changing his CD when he caught a glimpse of someone on the passenger side of his car. C-Bone just lit a joint when Felony said, "Watch out nigga," and C-Bone jumped when he saw the big 45 automatic pointed at him through the tinted car window as Little Tish started shooting, through the glass window.

The first and second bullet hit C-Bone in the face and head blowing his face all over the front seat. Felony punched on the gas puddle as two bullets hit him, one in the shoulder and the other skinned his back as he accelerated. The BMW shot forward and flew through the red light as a work truck filled with lawn mowers smashed right in the back of it, spinning it around twice before it hit the curve and stopped.

Little Tish saw Felony look up at her and he aimed his 9mm out of the window and started bussin' at her, as she started firing back at him. Princess saw Felony start shooting at Tish and she jumped out of the car and started bussin' at Felony too. Felony heard the bullets hitting his car door and he stepped back on the gas and swerve through traffic speeding off down the street.

Little Tish and Princess ran and jumped back in the car and Little Tish said, "Let's get that nigga and Princess throw the car in drive, and sped-off trying to catch-up with the BMW but it was no use, because Felony was gone.

"He's gone girl, let's get out of here before we get caught-up by the cops."

Princess and Little Tish made it home safe and called G-Fly and him and Julian stopped by so the girls could tell them what went down. After Princess explained what happened, they all were pumped up.

"Your crazy girl, you could've got killed like that." Julian scolded.

"Hell, I wasn't thinking about that, all I know is that I wanted to kill his punk ass, and I'm mad that I missed. But I got his homeboy. I know that I shot his punk ass too, I'm just mad that I didn't kill him!" Little Tish said.

"Well if nothing else, they know that we're not playing with their ass. They want a war, then we're going to give them a war." Julian said as he looked at Little Tish and smiled.

"Now this calls for a celebration. G-Fly said as he grabbed Princess big butt and squeezed it."

"Oh, you're horny huh? Lady-G got you on a pussy diet with those stitches in her. Huh?" said Princess.

"Damn bitch you must be psychic or something. Or was it the big bulge in my pants," G-Fly asked?

"Nope I'm psychic." Princess said as everybody started laughing.

"Oh, you got jokes too huh, well let's see if I can make you scream my name!" And G-Fly gave her that sexy look.

Little Tish give my nigga some of that bom pussy that you got. I'm sure he wants to show you his gratitude for your loyalty to him. You are still his ride or die bitch aren't you?" G-Fly asked as he tried to initiate the sexual desire between them.

"Of course I am!" Little Tish said as she giggled and looked at Julian and Julian blushed knowing that G-Fly just set him up.

"Well, take it easy on him, he's still kind of injured." G-Fly said as he laughed and followed Princess to her bedroom.

"Little Tish looked at Julian and said, "We ain't got to do anything, I know that you're down for me. I understand your feelings."

"Shut up and come and give me some of those pretty lips." Julian said as Little Tish blushed and melted in his arms.

* * * *

Felony called Monster to tell him what just happened.

"I'm telling you big homie, these muthafucka is crazy. A little bitch ran up on my shit shooting. She couldn't be no more then 18 or 19 years old. She blow C-Bone muthafucken face off and tried to kill me. I punched out, then after a truck ran into my shit, I pulled my shit out and started bussin' back at the bitch and she stood their while I was bussin' at her, and she started shooting back like she didn't give a fuck about me shooting at her. The bitch was fearless!" Felony said as he shook his head while holding the phone to his ear.

"Did you hit her," Monster asked.

"Hell naw, while we was shooting at each other, her home girl jumped out of her car and started bussin at me too. They got a crew of psycho bitches on their team." Felony muttered with conviction. "First Crime and Little Phil get's slumped, then this! Also, Gangsta and them went to put down a drive by, and they were ambushed. They said that they barely made it out of there."

"Chill out on this muthafucken phone nigga! I'ma talk to big bro and see what he wants to do. We probably got to send some of our little homies down there to air that muthafucka out. Better not let me find out that you're getting soft nigga!" Monster said in a pissed-off voice.

"Naw man, I'm just saying! I'm out numbered right now, and these young muthafucka's is crazy!"

"I'll get back at you, but in the mean time, find out what we need to know."

"I'm on it." Click, the phone went dead in Felony's ear as he shook his head and hung-up.

* * * *

G-Fly and Julian left the girls' baby mansion satisfied and feeling good. G-Fly was in his Bronco 4X4 rental truck as he pulled up to the Bank of America on Crenshaw Blvd. he looked over at Julian and said, "Here, hold this for me," and gave Julian his 45 automatic. "I'm going to deposit the money that we made from the club last week. I'll be back in a minute!"

"Cool," Julian said as he sat in the truck listening to his LL Cool J tape and singing the lyrics to G-Fly, "Tina had a big O' butt, I know I told you I'll be true, but Tina had a big O' butt, so I'm leaving you!"

G-Fly laughed and closed the truck door and walked into the bank to make his deposit.

"Hello Mr. Grant how may I help you today."

The teller merchant asked G-Fly as G-Fly vaguely laughed at the mention of his alias name. His mentor Game told him to always keep his business investments hidden in different alias name set up under different corporations. So if they ever get busted, then his wealth would be hidden from the Feds. "Well I want to make a deposit into my business account." G-Fly said with a professional smile.

"Sure Sir., what do we have here? Well I better get some help with this. Kim can you help me count this money please." Kim walked up and her eyes got big when she seen G-Fly.

G-Fly eyes deemed when he notice Kim and he reflected back to when him, Ty, and Julian meet Kim and Robin at the mall the day that they took their first new cars the 5.0, Iroc, and 300ZX to get hooked up at the rim and sound system shop. That was the same day that Julian met Tracy and the beginning of their journey into the game.

They took Kim and Robin out that night and ran across that punk ass nigga big Mike, and had to smash his ass in front of her, a quick end to their association. A lot has happened since then, but Kim poses no threat. G-Fly quickly ponder the situation then gave a little smile toward Kim. Kim looked nerves and started counting the money.

"Paula, I never seen that young lady here before, is she new?"

Paula, the older white teller looked over at Kim and said, "Oh yes, she just started a couple of days ago, but she's a quick learner!" Kim blushed and looked up at G-Fly for a hot minute, and then looked back down and continued counting the money.

Ten minutes later Paula said, "It comes up to $96,760 dollars Mr. Grant, is that correct?

"Yes, that's correct!"

"Well, here's your receipt sir."

"Thank you Maam," G-Fly said as he took the receipt looked at it, and put it in his pocket. Then he heard someone say, "Everybody get the fuck down on the ground!"

G-Fly looked back and saw four men with ski mask on and guns in their hands. G-Fly said, "Damn," then laid down on the cold marble floor.

Two of the bank robbers jump over the counter and started yelling, "Who's the manager? Who? Bring your ass over here, we're going to the vault and when we get there, you better have both the keys! You muthafuckas better not think about hitting no got damn buttons. Grab the keys and come on."

The bank manager grabbed the second pair of keys to the vault from the assistant manager and the robber grabbed the manager by the collar and lead him to the back.

The other robber was emptying out the teller's merchant drawers, and the other two robbers was in the lobby. One by the entrance door making people go lay down as they walked in, and the other walking back and forth in the lobby. G-Fly saw the robber slowly walked by him. Then ran over to a young buff white man who was across from G-Fly 15 feet away, and the robber kick the white man in the face and put his gun to the back of the buff white man's head and reached down and grabbed a gun from the buff white man's waist band. He looked down at the buff white man who was obviously an undercover cop, and started slapping him in the face and head with the big 357 magnum that he had in his hand. The buff white man was unconscious as the other bank robber ran from the back carrying two big duffle bags full of money and gave one to his abusive partner, as the third one caught up to them and they all ran out together watching each other backs.

Julian was changing his tape when he saw four mask men run out of the bank and jump into a green Chevy and burned rubber down the street as they sped away. "What the fuck!" Julian said as his thoughts were moving a thousand miles a minute. He started stashing the guns in the Bronco and sat back down as police cars started coming from all direction. Julian laughed to himself and said, "To late sucka's" then smiled!

G-Fly and Julian was briefly interrogated then allowed to leave the bank with the other customers. "Ain't that that bitch Kim that we met at the mall awhile back?" Julian asked as he peep her when she was getting interrogated by the police.

"Yep, that's her….she just started working there a couple of days ago." G-Fly remarked as he drove out of the bank parking lot.

"I wonder did she have anything to do with it." Julian questioned?

"I really doubt it, considering that her friend tried it once before, and it didn't turn out to good for her." G-Fly said as he made an expressive facial expression allow Julian to remember what happen to Jackie after Big Mike robbed her bank.

"Yea, you're probably right! Anyway, what happen in there?"

"Man that shit was off the hook! These muthafucka came storming in with guns drawn and telling everyone to lay down and shit. It was like the movies."

"Did you lie down?" Julian asked knowing that G-Fly always is playing like he's so hard and stuff.

"You're muthafucken right I laid down on that cold ass floor! I was probably the first person on the ground." They both started busting up laughing. G-Fly grabbed his cigarette lighter and blast a joint.

"Where's my shit at?"

"Oh, I had to stash it when I heard all of those police sirens." Julian said as he reached under the interior arm rest and pulled both of the guns out.

"Here!" Julian handed him his gun and G-Fly gave Julian the joint.

"Anyway, as those muthafuckas was putting the lick down, this big stupid-ass white man was moving funny while he was on the ground and one of the rubbers ran over and kicked him right in the fuckin face, then reaches down and grabbed a gun from the dude's waist band. Then he started beating the shit out of him with this big ass 357 magnum. I mean splitting his shit to the white meat. At that point I was frozen on the floor, because I sure didn't want to get fucked up like that!" And they both started rollin. "After that, one of the robbers the one that went into the vault, came running out with two big duffle bags full of money, then the other one who was cleaning out the teller draws and the teller's merchant draw, ran by and caught up to the other three, and they all backed out while the forth one was looking out the door and they all ran out together." G-Fly said as he finished up the story.

"Man, all I saw was four guys with ski mask run out and jumped into a green Chevy and roll out. I didn't even see them run in, they must've been on top of their game."

"Hell yea, they were professionals. And they had to hit for about close to a ticket!" G-Fly said.

"You think so?" "Man I'm telling you, them bags was pregnant." They started laughing as G-Fly turned into the drive way of their mansion.

They got out of the truck and walked into the mansion and was greeted by Lady-G and the baby. "Hey honey, look little G there goes daddy and uncle J." Lady-G said as she walked up and kissed G-Fly and said, "Oooowow, you smell like Princess," and

Julian started bustin' up laughing as he gave Lady-G a kiss on the cheek and kissed little G on the head.

"Damn girl, you're like one of those blood hounds! I took a shower and everything….It's good that I'm a player or I'd be busted."

"Fuck you G-Fly, that's not funny nigga." Lady-G said as she poked out her lips.

"Shit you should be happy, because I was on the verge of busting those stitches!" And they all started bustin' up.

"You think your slick nigga!"

"Not slick but Fly baby, just Fly to the bone." G-Fly smiled and kissed her on the lips then gave little G a kiss on his head and said, "Your going to be a boss player like your daddy huh!"

"He is not going to be a player, he's going to be a doctor."

"Anyway, guess what!" Lady-G said.

"What baby, quit playing!"

"O'kay, I went over to my auntee Joyce's house today to show her little G, and my cousin was there home from the Army. He got kicked out on some disobeying a direct order shit. Anyway, he's been in the army like 10 years and was with a special force squad, some Rambo shit. He fucked up and they kicked his ass out, so he ain't got a job or nothing.

After kicking it with him for a minute, I told him that we were in the middle of a war against some other dope dealers."

"You told him that?" G-Fly said in an angry tone.

"Yea, he knows what I'm into, he knew Game real good, and he put in some work for Game one time when he was home on a short leave. That's what he does, he's a trained killer. A couple of years ago his little brother got gun down by the police on some scandalous shit, and his little brother died. Game paid for the funeral and moved his mother into a nice house in Pomona, so she could raise her other two kids in a better environment. Anyway he had a lot of respect and love for Game, and after we talked, he wanted to know can he work for us? I told him that it was a deadly game and he said, "That's the only way that he knows how to play!"

"Man I don't know about this shit!" G-Fly said as he looked at Julian for his input.

"Listen baby, all you got to do is talk to him and feel him out, and if you like him and could relate to him, then hook him up with something. What better weapon to have in a time of war then a trained assassin."

"Lady-G might be onto something." Julian said as he contemplated his thoughts. "This nigga obviously been trained by the best and his skills might come in handy if we can set him up with the right equipment and shit. We might need to start a small investigation agency, and by him the equipment so he can keep tabs on certain people and watch our backs. That way, we can be a step in front of our enemies, and anybody who opposed us."

"That's smart but what if he gets busted after he put's down a couple of hits. How do we know if he'll keep it G? You know that the Army brainwash muthafuckas!"

"Well baby, how do we know that anyone who gets down with us is going to keep it 100% real when the shit hits the fan? I know that Kevin hates cops, and I know that he's down and a trained killer. I rather have him on my team, then 5 street gangsters anytime, because I know that he knows how to take a muthafucka' out right. And if we catch heat from the big boys, then we got someone who we know can get the job done right," Lady-G said.

"She has a point!" Julian said as Ty walked in.

"What's good my niggas?"

"Well, first of all….your sister found us an assassin that she wants to bring into the family to be our personal hit man." G-Fly said as he looked over at Lady-G and she smiled back at him.

"That's a good idea, we need someone with some skills to stack the deck. Is he good," Ty asked?

G-Fly looked surprised as Julian and Lady-G laughed. "She said that the niggas is like Rambo!" G-Fly said in a sarcastic tone.

"Well that what we need, a super killer so we can put an end to this shit and get back to making money." Ty expressed as he smiled at Julian.

"Well, I guess that we need to set up a meeting with him," said Julian.

"Good, I'll go call him and tell him to come on by." Lady-G said as she sat little G in his car seat and put him next to G-Fly.

"Hey little man," G-Fly said to little G as he yawned and closed his eyes.

"Guess what Ty?"

"What?"

"G-Fly was caught up in a bank robbery!" Julian said with a look of excitement on his face.

"What," Ty said as he looked at G-Fly for conformation.

"Yea my nigga, they came in with guns and ski masks and laid the whole bank down."

"You're bullshitting."

"No I'm not, I was….. and G-Fly went on to tell Ty and Lady-G about the bank robbery from start to finish.

Chapter 6
Know Thy Enemies

Lady-G's cousin Kevin arrived at the mansion about 7:30 that evening and G-Fly, Ty, Julian and Lady-G all sat at the big long black marble table which they referred to as the round table. This was where all of their secret meetings and serious decision got debated and decided on. Julian passed the joint to G-Fly and looked at Kevin and asked, "So what type of work did you do in the Army?"

"Well I was with a Special Forces Black Ops Team, we dealt with important secret missions, basically infiltrate and destroy our enemies."

"You mean like the A-Team!" Ty asked?

"Yea, similar to them, but we had more complex missions."

"What type of special skills do you have?" Asked G-Fly in a interrogating way.

"Well, I'm a sharp shooter, with demolition experience and I'm a combat specialist."

"What do that mean?" asked G-Fly.

"Well, I can shoot a fly off a horse's ass from over a hundred yards away, and I know how to use explosives also, I know Judo, Martial Arts, Tae-Kwon-du, and Combat-do. Kevin said with a smug smile on his face.

"What's Combat-do," Julian asked?

"It's a technique used to specifically kill your opponent!" Kevin stated.

"Damn, that vicious! Looks like we got a muthafucken super nigga here!" G-Fly said as he smiled at his comrades. Listen "Coman-bro," G-Fly said as everyone started busting up. "We're caught up in a different type of war here! We're a family that's down and loyal to one another in every aspect of this game. We ride together, kill together, and ready to die together at a drop of a dime. We don't give a damn about no muthafucken cops. If they oppose us or try to harm us in anyway, then will kill them. Now if you can't live with this or the punishment that would come with doing something like this, then you need to leave now and save yourself some problems."

Everyone looked at Kevin for a reply and he smiled at them and said, "I'm down for what-ever, just tell me what you need done, and I'll make it happen."

G-Fly past Kevin the joint and he hesitated at first then took it and hit it and started coughing." You can't be a dope fend coughing like that!" And everyone started laughing as Ty took the joint from Kevin.

"So tell us, why did you get kicked out of the Army," G-Fly asked?

"We were on a mission in Iran looking for this terrorist, when we got word that he was hiding out at a Mosque. We set up a perimeter around the Mosque to prevent anyone from being able to escape. A bus full of women and children left the Mosque and my lieutenant colonel gave me and my unit the order to blow the bus up. Me and my sergeant had rocket launchers that could've easily blown-up the bus and killed everyone on board, but I refuse to blow up the bus loaded with innocent women and children, nor could my sergeant do it, so we both got court marshaled for disobeying a direct order, and received a dishonorable discharge and basically kicked out." Kevin said as he looked up from his trance and stared at G-Fly straight in the eyes.

"Well it's good to know that you got pride and dignity about yourself. But we're up against niggas that's of the lowest form of animals. These nigga killed my brother Julian's fiancée who was eight months pregnant with his seed. They shot her in the stomach three times with no remorse. So now my question to you is, if you have to kill this nigga while he's in the car with his family, can you do it?" G-Fly asked Kevin as he looked him back straight into his eyes.

Kevin contemplated the thought for a minute, then said, "as long as they're not on a bus full of innocent women and children then he's fair game." And everyone smiled at Kevin's reply.

"O'kay Kevin, why don't you go have a seat in the living room and help yourself to the bar while we contemplate our thoughts.

"O'kay, Mr. Julian," Kevin said as he got up and walked out of the room and shut the door behind himself.

"So what do you guys think about him," Lady-G asked?

"I think that he's most definitely an asset! He got heart, skills, he's smart and looks as square as they come," Ty said.

"Yea, I agree! Julian said, we can establish a security and private eye service for him, so he can have an employment front. And we'll buy a limousine and a big Chevy truck so he can use it for his business. We can also buy all that spy equipment so he can use it for surveillance. Hook him up with Jason so he can get the guns that he needs and put his ass to work. He shouldn't have any problems getting a gun license to carry." Julian expressed as everyone listened to his game plan.

"I like it", G-Fly said, "we can let him stay in the house in Inglewood and let him hire some employees for the business, so it can be legit and not draw any unwanted attention."

"That's a good idea my niggas. I wonder if any of the soldiers that were in his unit are still around." Ty said as he looked at Lady-G.

"We can ask him?" Lady-G said.

"Well, is it a go or what ya'll," Ty asked?

Julian, "It's good with me."

"I guess it's final then," G-Fly said as he looked over at Lady-G and said, "you can go call him back in!"

"O'kay baby!" And Lady-G walked out to get Kevin.

Kevin walked back in trailing Lady-G. "Kevin, your new nick name is Big Bro!" G-Fly said as everyone started laughing and clapping. "Welcome home my nigga." Everyone stood up and gave him a ghetto embrace.

"I have a question?" Ty said. "What happen to the other soldier that was in your unit?"

"Well me and my sergeant took the blame and got kicked out, and everyone else just got split up and went on about their lives." Kevin said.

"Well if your sergeant got the same mentality and understanding as you, then see if he needs employment."

"I'll check on it."

"O'kay listen Big Bro, we're going to establish a Security and Private Investigation Service for you so you can have a legitimate front to work in. You can hire any employees you want to help you operate the business. We're also going to buy you a limousine so that you can drive around in it and look good for the business and a big Chevy truck to keep your private eye equipment in. We have a house in Inglewood in a nice quiet neighborhood that you can live in.

Now, we have an associate who sells all kinds of guns, and can hook you up to get what ever you need.

We'll decided to start you off at 100g's a year, for your service to us, and will cut you in for half of whatever profit the Security and Private Investigation Service earns. We'll need to rent you a business office so you can look all the way legit," G-Fly said.

"Do you know where to get you're private eye equipment at," Julian asked?

"Yep!"

"Good then, will give you 50g's so that you can go buy what you need, and get yourself some new clothes so that you can stay sharp. We like that square look that you got going-on, so try not to change your look to much. Lady-G will take you by your new house in Inglewood and go get you a pager to stay in contact. Then tomorrow we'll go shop for a nice limousine and Chevy truck for you, and then take you to buy some guns and shit for the business."

Ty walked back in the room and placed a black duffle bag in front of Kevin. "That's 50g's in there, that should help you get the equipment that you need and buy you some nice clothes."

"Thank you Sir!"

"Big Bro, you don't have to call us Sir., your family now, so address us by our street names. It sounds more formal."

G-Fly said as everyone smiled.

"O'kay Sir., I mean G-Fly!"

"I guess that an old habit is hard to break, huh?" G-Fly said as he grabbed a joint from the weed box and lit it.

"I'll smoke to that," Ty said, "put it in the air!"

* * * *

"Listen nigga, I'm paying more for this shit now, so I got to go up on my prices. I need $650 dollars off every ounce now."

"Damn, that's a whole $150 dollars more." Tim Tim said.

"Yo, nigga I can't help it! It's a drought now, and this war is fucking off my paper. If you don't want to get money no more, then just let me know and I'll go get some other homies who's trying to get paid to work this spot.

"Fuck it, I'll give you the $650 dollars, but these rocks is about to go on a diet." Tim Tim said as him and Dre gave each other dap and laughed.

"As long as you don't dog the clientele, then I don't give a damn what you do." Wheels said as he handed Tim Tim and Dre three ounces a piece.

* * * *

Princess, Dee Dee, Gwen and Little Tish was all at Julian's mother beauty salons getting their hair and nails hooked up when Princess and Gwen over heard two stripper girls talking about the birthday party that they were hired that night to dance at. The big booty light skin girl said that it was for a baller nigga out of Compton. Princess eyes got big as she looked over at Gwen and Gwen gave her that look!

"Excuse me ladies, ooowow, I love your shoes." Princess said to break the ice.

"Thank you." One of the stripper's said with a friendly smile.

"Listen I don't mean to be all up in your business, but I over heard you talking about doing a birthday party for some baller niggas out of Compton." Princess said as the girl defenses went up.

"Yea, what about it?"

"Well, I own an escort service myself and a while back a baller nigga from Compton hooked up with one of my girls, he hired her to dance for a birthday party and when she got their, she said that it was twelve niggas their and after she did her dance number, they beat her up and raped her, then told her that they will kill her if she tried to tell the police anything about it. They gave her claps, crabs, and violated her big butt numerous time." Princess said then looked down at the light skin girl's big ass.

"That's crazy! Are you serious?"

"Yea girl, I wouldn't lie about no shit like that, but I don't know if it's the same niggas."

"Well the nigga that I met was named Gino, and he said that it was for his big homie named Big Rob, Big Felony, or some shit like that." The light skin girl said with a curious look on her face.

"Yep that's them....I tell you what? How much are they going to pay you to dance for them," Princess asked?

"Their going to pay us five hundred dollars a piece."

"Well I'll tell you what....I'll give you both Twelve hundred dollars a piece to buy this contract from ya'll, and you tell me where they want ya'll to meet them at, and I'ma send my security crew over their to make sure that they don't get away with disrespecting my girl."

"That's right, I'm down with that," and the big booty light skin girl looked at her friend. Her friend said, "Hell yea, I wasn't gonna go anyway, after hearing what them sorry niggas did to your friend."

Princess smiled and reached into her Gucci purse and pulled out a big wod of money and counted out two twelve hundred dollars stacks and handed one to both of the girls. "Now where are you girls supposed to meet them at," Princess asked?

"They got a room at the Best Western Motel on Western Blvd. Room 187 and we're suppose to meet them there at seven o'clock tonight.

"O'kay, how did you meet Gino?"

"I worked at First King Strip Club on Western and he came in with a couple of his homeboys flashing big bank rolls and tricking. We kicked it, and I gave him a lap dance and he told me about the party and asked me if I wanted to make some money dancing for his homeboys c-day party, as he called it. I agreed and I gave him my pager number and he called me today and told me to get one of my cute friends with a big butt," (and they both looked over at her brown skin thick friend who also had a big butt.)

"Hell naw, ain't no butty sex going on here!" Her friend said as they all laughed.

"Anyway, he told me to meet him at the Best Western Motel at 7:00 o'clock tonight and gave me the room number. I hope this shit don't come back on me." The light skin girl said with a eerie look in her eyes.

"You really don't have to worry about that! I guarantee you. Gino won't be looking for any more strippers after my people get through with him," Princess said.

"Well listen, if you need some extra girls to dance for you some times, then call me, here is my pager number. They call me Sexy."

"O'kay Sexy, and I hope that this little issue stay between us."

"Of course, any nigga who be doing that kind of stuff to ladies, deserve to get fucked up." And they all laughed as Little Tish and Dee-Dee walked up and Princess and Gwen stood up and said their good-byes.

* * * *

That same day G-Fly and Julian took Big Bro to buy the limousine and new truck, then met with Jason the arms dealer. "J., Fly what's good my young gangsters?" Jason greeted them with a friendly smile and a ghetto hand shake. Jason was a white boy who was raised around blacks, so he was as hipped as they come.

"What's up hustler? G-Fly said as he turned and said this is our new bodyguard, we brought him to get his shit right."

"Cool, cool, I trust you Fly, Jason said as he looked at Big Bro suspicious with that Army hair-cut looking like an undercover cop! "Come on in the back room and check out the stash." Jason said as he directed them to his back room.

Big Bro walked into the back room and eyes instantly lit up. Julian handed him some brownie gloves and said, "Help yourself."

Big Bro was like a kid in a candy store. He grabbed a Tec 9 looked at it and said, "Give me two of these." He grabbed a AR-15 rifle and said, "I'll take three of these." He grabbed a 30-30 rifle with a scope on it and looked at Jason and said, "Do you have any silencers for this?"

"Yes, I got silencers for almost everything except that big shit" and he pointed at the AR-15, AK-47 and HK-17.

"O'kay I'll take two of these with the scope and silencers. Give me two Mac10's with the silencers too, two of the 12 gages with the pistol grip, two of those 45 automatics with silencers, 4 9mm with silencers, two of those rocket launchers, and 4 bullet proof vests." He stopped and looked at the youngsters and they all smiled.

"Anything else," Jason asked?

"Yea give me 8 of those new 9mm, 8 of those new 45 automatics, and ammo for all of them and throw in 8 more of those bullet proof vests. Those damn things come in handy." G-Fly said then smiled.

"That all comes up to $32,800 dollars." Ty opened up a brief case full of money and started laying down stacks of money as he counted it out.

They loaded up Big Bro's new truck and followed him to his new house in Inglewood.

While they were unloaded the guns at Big Bro's new house, G-Fly got a page from Princess. Princess told him about the stripper bitches that they met at Momma's J beauty salon, and the conversation that transpired. G-Fly told her that he'll call her back and then looked at Julian, Ty, and Big Bro and then said, "Today might be our lucky day." Julian and Ty's eyes got big as G-Fly told them how Princess ran into some stripper bitches at your Mom's beauty salon and that they was hired to do a birthday party for that nigga Felony and his homeboy's at the Best Western on Western Blvd. They told the girls that Felony and his homeboy's raped and beat up one of her friends, and that she wanted to pay them back. Princess paid the bitches for their loss and the bitch gave Princess the room number and time that they suppose to show up. So the next move is on us."

"O'kay, we got to make this move count! Julian said, as they all started brainstorming. Didn't Princess say that they were expecting strippers to show up? Julian asked as everyone smiled but Big Bro.

Big Bro looked at all of them and said, "What?"

"Well, I don't think that we mentioned that we own an escort service of some of the baddest and finest bitches that money can buy." G-Fly said as he looked at Julian and Ty and said, "I'll call Lady-G!"

Ty looked at Big Bro and said, "Well it's time to show and prove my nigga."

G-Fly called Lady-G and told her the situation and what he needed, then he called Princess back and told her his plan, and for them to meet up at the youngster's main mansion.

* * * *

Gino, OG Frog, Kilo-C, MD, Tank, Big Rob, Loc, Too-Too, BK, Cubin and Big-G were all in the Best Western Motel smoking weed and drinking celebrating Big Rob's c-day.

They were waiting for Gino's big surprise which everyone knew was some strippers and also, they were waiting for Felony to show up with his big surprise as well.

They heard a knock on the door and GO Frog opened it and seen five bad bitches standing there wearing black trench coats and each had on a cat-woman mask in red three inch stiletto heels.

"Damn, come in ladies, come in."

"Is this where the birthday party at?" One of the ladies asked.

"You muthafucken right it is." OG Frog said as the ladies walked in.

All the men were drooling as the ladies walked in "Hold up! Gino said who are ya'll?"

"We're the birthday boy entertainment!" One of the ladies said.

"Where's Sexy?"

"Man fuck Sexy!" Tank said as he stared at the bad Cubin looking bitch.

"She couldn't make it.... It's that time of the month thing, if you know what I mean! Do you want us to dance for you guys or what?"

"Hell yea!" Big Rob said as one of the ladies flirted with him.

"O'kay, but I'm only paying a thousand dollars like me and Sexy agreed upon."

"As long as ya'll tip well we're cool with that, now is it somewhere we can go get ready at?"

"Yea, the bathroom," Gino said.

"O'kay, ya'll kick back and get ready for a performance to remember." One of the ladies said as they walked into the bathroom.

Once in the bathroom the ladies reached into the two purses that they had with them and pulled out two 9mm, two 3.80 automatics, and one big 45 automatic all equipped with silencers. All the ladies looked over at the big 45 automatic that Little Tish had and laughed. "Shit, I came to put it down!" Said Little Tish with a smile on her face.

"Listen, on three we go out and smoke everything in here, one, two, three!"

"Everybody was telling Gino how bad the bitches were that he selected, and when the bathroom door opened up all of them looked toward the bathroom and saw the ladies come out in slow motion as Princess shot BK twice in the head with the 9mm then shot Kilo-C four times in the chest. Everybody jumped up trying to run and Lil Tish shot Loc three times in his stomach and once in the head. MD swung on Princess and Princess jumped out of the way as Treasure the youngster's down Cubin and the bitch shot MD four times in the face dropping him dead.

Big G ran and jumped out of the window with Too-Too right behind him, and when he jumped Gwen shot him five times in the back. Gino went for his 357 magnum that he had in his waist band and Lil Tish and Dee-Dee both unloaded on him then shot OG and Frog, too.

Big Rob sat at the table smoking his joint watching the slaughter take place, as Princess drew down on him and he just grinned as Princess shot him right between the eyes killing him dead. Then she looked back at Dee-Dee and said, "Go get the purses," and Dee-Dee ran back into the bathroom to grab the purses while Lil Tish, Gwen, and Treasure was shooting everyone in the head to make sure that they were dead, then they walked out and Dee-Dee looked down at Too-Too laid out on the ground outside the window and shot him twice as they walked to the car that was parked on the side with Big Bro sitting in the driver seat.

They walked up and saw Big-G lying dead along side the car and Lil Tish shot Big-G one more time," then jumped in the car and Big Bro drove off.

Ty and Julian were parked at one end of the Motel and G-Fly was parked at the other end, and they all drove off back to back trailing each other. After they drove about three blocks away, the ladies jumped out of the car with Big Bro and into the cars with Julian and Ty and G-Fly. Big Bro took the G-ride into an alley where they had decided to burn it. Then he walked out of the alley and around the block and jumped into a rent-a-car that was parked there and drove off to meet the youngsters at the main mansion.

* * * *

After Big Bro and them pulled away, Felony pulled up in his new Cadillac Fleetwood Brougham. "What the fuck!" Felony said as he seen Too-Too laid outside the motel room window twisted in a puddle of blood.

Felony surprise for Big Rob's birthday, was that he was bringing Little Creep and Monster to his party. Then they were going to take him out and show him a good time. Little Creep and Monster jumped out of the car with guns drawn running toward the room as Felony ran behind them watching their backs. Once they got inside the motel room and looked in Little Creep said, "What the Fuck, Who did this shit?"

"Damn Boss I don't know!" Monster said.

"It had to be those muthafucken youngster boss, I told ya'll that they were some crazy muthafuckas." Felony said as he shook his head with disbelief.

"Let's go Boss before the cops arrive, we can't get caught up on this one!" Monster said as he pulled Little Creep away from the scene and they got back into the Cadillac and drove off just then they saw Big G face down off to the side in the parking lot. Felony stopped for a couple of seconds as they gazed at Big G's body then Monster said, "Let's roll." Felony pulled off and jumped back on the freeway headed back toward Compton.

Little Creep said, "Monster I want you on this one! Grab whoever you need, and kill all of these young niggas and their crazy bitches."

"Yes boss, I'm on it." Monster said as Felony knew that the shit just hit the fan.

Chapter 7
Never Trust A Big Butt and A Smile

The youngster spent a couple of days partying and getting thing back on track. The ladies hit was well planned out and the massacre was all over the news. The police called it a gang affiliated war and the governor vowed to crack down on all drug and gang activity in the city.

The youngster's order Princess and the ladies to just handle the outer city clientele; with the exception of Killa and his homeboys.

The youngsters got word that Wheels was copping work from a different source and was pissed off. They decided to disaffiliate themselves with him and let him have his blocks, rock house, and territory for himself. G-Fly wanted to kill him for being disloyal to them, but Ty and Julian voted against it, and decided that they no longer wanted to waste their time on crack houses and crack spot.

Princess would only sell weight to their elite clientele in bulk, and she was glad that Wheels got cut off, because she didn't like the way his attitude changed since he started getting money.

Ty was taking the 30 kilos that he had at one of the stash house, to the other stash house that Princess and the ladies had access to. The youngster's got it set up in away that they'll be the only ones who have access to the stash house that held the majority of dope. So the youngsters would transport, give or take, 50 kilos at a time to the stash house that Princess and the ladies had access too, and the ladies would get a page from their clients and go get the work that they order and take it to them.

* * * *

Ty was in his new Grand National black on black with light tinted windows when the police got behind him and hit their lights. "Damn, Damn, Damn." Ty cursed as he looked over in the passenger seat at the black duffle bag filled with cocaine. He pulled over and saw two white police exiting their police car. The passenger cop shielded himself behind the police vehicle door, while his partner the driver, started walking up on the Grand National with his hand on his gun. Ty thoughts raced as he timed it, and as soon as the police got 10 feet away from his police vehicle, then Ty punched it, burning rubber as the Grand National took off. The police ran back to his vehicle and got in hot pursuit.

Ty laughed as the Grand National sped-away with lighting speed making distance between him and the police vehicle. He knew that he had to act fast because cops where all over the ghetto neighborhoods of Los Angeles.

He turned on Long Beach Blvd and punched it and the Grand National hit a 110 mph instantly, he saw the police vehicle hit the corner about a block in the rear of him, so he turned on 53rd and passed up a police vehicle going in the opposite direction, they hit their brakes and busted a u-turn and almost hit the other police car as both police vehicle skidded to a halt, then punched back out after the Grand National. Ty turned on Homes and drove into the parking lot of the Pueblo Projects, where the Notorious Pueblo Bishop Blood dwelt. It was niggas, women, kids, and smokers all over the place. Ty pulled up by some young game members and two of the young bloods pulled guns as Ty said, "Hold up player, here take this bag," and he opened up his car door and threw out the big duffle bag full of cocaine and closed the door, then punched back out and threw his gun out as he drove to the other side of the parking lot, and the police vehicle blocked him off in every direction. Ty jumped out of the car and laid on the ground before the police could jump out of their car, so they ran over to him with guns drawn and jumped on his back and hand cuffed him, then they started to punch him and kick him in the body and face. Two shots from a gun went off and hit the Grand National back window 10 feet away from where Ty was getting his ass wooped.

The police looked up and saw a big crowd of people and lifted Ty up and throw him in the back of the police car then jumped into their vehicles and backed out of the projects, and drove away with Ty in the back seat of their police car.

Ty saw that every body was crowding the parking lot so the cops couldn't identify the shooter, so they grabbed their criminal and left out of the projects. The residence that lived in the Pueblo Project was known for being hard on cops, they were a community of ghetto families who kept it ghetto all the way, and the cops knew that the shooter was giving them a warning shot; the next shot would've been fatal. And if the policemen were foolish enough to shoot back, then every Blood gang-banger that was in the Project's that day would've opened fire.

"I hope that you don't think that I'm finished with whoppin' your ass nigger! You almost got us killed twice, and that pissed me all the way off." The big buff red-neck cop said as he turned around in the passenger seat staring at Ty through the steal gate that separated them.

"What's your damn name?"

"Joseph Roberts," Ty said, giving his alias name that's on his driver's licenses.

The cop ran Ty's name and nothing came up, he consider that if Ty didn't have any prior records coming up it would be hard for him to kick his prisoner ass in custody and get away with it.

"Do you have a criminal record?"

"No Sir,"

"Then why did you run when we pulled you over?"

"Why did you pull me over?" Ty asked as the police began to turned red in the face and replied, "Oh, you want to get smart with me huh, will see how tuff you are when we get you down to the County Jail." He said with a bull-shit laugh.

They took Ty to the County Jail and stripped searched him. And when the cops didn't find anything, they got mad. They put Ty in a holding cell by himself and immediately Ty jumped on the phone and made a call to the house.

The phone rung and Lady-G picked up the phone on the second ring.

"Hello!"

"You have a collect call from a Joseph Roberts, if you accept it the cost will be $2.50 for the first minute and $1.25 for each additional minute after that. If you accept? Please press 5, if not then hung up." Lady-G pressed 5.

"Hello," Ty said.

"Hey baby, where are you?"

"I'm at the L.A. County Jail."

"What's your bail?"

"I don't know, they haven't' charged me with anything yet!"

"O'kay, Ron will be their shortly, are you Ok?"

"They whopped my ass a bit, but I'll survive!"

"They did what! You just relax baby, I'ma make some phone calls O'kay!"

"O'kay sis, holler! Ty said as he hung up the phone and sat down on the cold block of cement.

The Lieutenant and police detectives were in the office with the four policemen as the officers explained what happened.

"Let me get this straight the detectives said, so you're telling me that you pulled this vehicle over and he waited for you to get out of your car then sped-off! You jumped back into your vehicle and got in hot pursuit of his vehicle as he turned into the Pueblo Projects, then jumped out and laid down on the ground as you four surrounded him and placed him in hands cuffs. Then you guys heard gun shots and saw the back of his car window shatter. So you picked him up and placed him in your vehicle then drove off because you felt that your lives were in jeopardy."

"That sounds about right, sir!" The big buff redneck cop said.

"Well are you guys sure that you wasn't putting your hands on that boy before the shots were fired at you in the parking lot," the detective asked?

"He was kind of resisting arrest a bit, so we had to wrestle with him a little bit," the cop replied.

"Well how do you explain the bruises on his face?"

"He must've already been like that!" The cop said as he shrugged his shoulders.

"Well can you please tell me what happen to his got-damn car? When they went to tow it away, it wasn't there anymore. So let me get this straight! We got a high speed chase but no car, someone allegedly shot at you and the bullet hit his car window, but being that we have no car, we also have no evidence of a shooting! But we got a young man in the holding cell with bruises all over his face and body, and he has no fucking criminal record. So tell me Officer Davis, what can we charge this young man with?"

"Sir., fleeing arrest and assaulting an officer." Officer Davis said in his defense.

The Captain walked in and said, "I just got a call from the Governor of California talking about a police abuse case that happened in the Pueblo Projects today and I had another phone call from Attorney Ron Johnson? Do you know who Attorney Ron Johnson is, he will have this whole damn police force under federal investigation." The Captain said as he looked around at everybody in the room. Will someone tell me what the hell is going on?"

"Well it seems like Officer Davis here and his partner Officer Smith got into a high speed chase with that young man in the holding tank his name is Joseph Roberts. Mr. Roberts' lead the high speed chase into the Pueblo Projects where the subject got out of his car and laid face down on the ground surrendering to police when he realize that he was cornered. Officer Davis said that he resisted some in the beginning which lead to them having to use a bit of force. At which time two shots were let off that shattered the car window that the suspect was driving. Then they saw a crowd of hostile people approaching so they detained the suspect then fled the scene."

"Where's the car at," the Captain asked?

"Well someone stole it from the scene of the crime and we got an APB on it now." The Lieutenant answered.

"Does he have any criminal record?"

"No Sir., his name came up clean."

"How bad are his physical wounds?" The Captain asked in an aggressive tone!

"They're 45 percent noticeable!"

The Captain looked at the four offices and said, "I want your reports on my desk in two hours, and take the rest of the week off! You better pray that this incident blow away without any political attention." The four police officers looked at each other as the Captain walked out of the room with the Detective following close behind him. The Captain needed something to go on, so he sent the Detective into the investigation room to interview Ty.

The County Jail officer brought Ty into the waiting room to be interviewed by the Detective. The Detective walked in and said, "How are you doing Mr. Roberts?" Ty just sat there staring at the Detective with a blank facial expression.

"I want to ask you about the high speed chase. Why did you run from the police," the Detective asked?

"I would like for my attorney to be present!" Ty firmly stated.

"Well, we might decide not to press charges on you Sir."

"Listen I want to speak to my attorney! I know my rights and I wish to invoke them." Ty stated with big eyes. With that he heard a knock on the two way mirror as the Detective looked at Ty and smiled, then got up and left.

Ty's attorney Ron Johnson arrived within the hour and all charges was dropped against Ty, and the Captain could only hope that the youngster didn't file a law suit against the police department. But Ty wasn't as forgiving, and told his attorney Ron to go ahead and file the law suit and to put a restraining order on the Los Angeles police department. Ron was happy to, as they shook hands and Ty jumped into the car with Lady-G and drove away.

Ty told Julian, G-Fly and Lady-G everything that had happened and they all had a good laugh that ran late into the night.

* * * *

Wheel's was at his plush condo located on the Westside off Crenshaw enjoying some of the best head that he ever had from Evett sexy big butty ass, when he heard a knock on the door. Damn who can this be? He said to himself as he looked at Evett fine ass sitting there in a thong on with her 36C titties looking fat to death. "Don't move baby." He said as he put his dick back in his boxers and went to see who was at his door. He peeped out of the peep hole and saw this cute light skin sista standing outside his door.

"Who is it?"

"Ummm, my name is Nicky and I just backed into the Blue Astro Van with the gold rims on it, and someone said that it was yours!"

Wheels eyes got big as he opened up the door and when he was opening it, someone pushed the front door real hard and two mask men ran into his condo with guns drawn. "What's this?" He said as one of

102

the mask men slapped him in the face with a big ass
357 magnum.

Nicky hollered! As the other mask man grabbed
her by the hair and throw her on the ground and put
his 45 automatic to her head and said, "If you scream
one more time then it will be your last! Do you
understand me?" Nicky shook her head yes! "Who
else is in here?" The mask man asked Nicky.

"I don't know?"

They hand cuffed Wheels and Nicky and said,
"Now listen nigga we can do this the easy way or the
hard way. Where is the dope and the money at?"

Wheels briefly contemplated his options then
said, "It's in the bedroom closet in the safe and duffle
bag. The combination is 7-2-11...!" then the mask
robber walked into the bedroom with his pistol
drawn. He unzipped the duffle bag and saw seven
kilos, and then he opened-up the safe and saw stacks
of money. He grabbed a pillow case off the bed and
filled it up with money.

Then he started searching the room and no one
else was there. Evett had jump out of the window
naked when she heard the robbers push through the
front door.

As the robber searched the room he found a 9mm,
a Tech 9, and some jewelry. Then he walked back out
and put the pillow case with the money and duffle
bag that had the dope by the front door. His
homeboy smiled and asked, "was it good?"

"Yep, it was nice! Just like her fine ass." Nicky
looked up at him scared.

"Oh, you like that huh?" One mask man said to
the other as the other one grabbed his dick through
his pants and licked his lips.

"Go ahead, we got time and some condoms is right here on the table."

"Man, you got what you came for, just take the money and dope and leave!"

"Shut the fuck up punk before we smoke your stupid ass." One robber said as he unzipped his jeans and pulled out his dick on rock hard and slid the rubber on.

"Please don't do this to me." Nicky bagged as the robber slapped her hard across the face and said, "shut the fuck up, and you better fuck me good or I'ma kill your pretty ass do you here me?"

Nicky shook her head as the robber pulled down her red thong and licked his lips as he seen her fat bald pussy lips smile at him, then he slid all the way in with one push and started fucking her hard and fast. She fucked back like a pro and he came in three minutes flat. He rolled off and smiled up at his partner and said, "she got the bom!"

"Is that right well I better see for myself," the other robber said as he pulled out a 10 inch big fat dick and stretched a rubber around it as Nicky looked on with tears in her eyes as he straddle her and slid in slowly as he started fucking her slow and passionately. She was breathing hard and fucking back as he took his time and watched as her eyes rolled back into her head and she pumped faster as she had an orgasm. He laughed and said, "Oh, you like this bom dick huh?" she bite down on her lower lip to try to fight back the sensation. He put her legs up to her chest and started long stroking her as she moaned in pleasure, then he felt his nut coming so he started fucking her faster as she screamed in ecstasy and they both came together as both of their bodies tensed up then relaxed. "Damn baby, to bad we didn't meet under different circumstances. However, since that pussy was so good, we're not going to kill you guys. So consider this you're lucky day." Then he laughed as he threw the hand cuff key behind the couch and he and his partner grabbed the pillow case and the duffle bag and walked out the door.

"Wheels was able to retrieve the key from behind the couch and unhand cuffed himself and Nicky. Nicky cried as she ran and jump in the shower. Wheels was mad, but he felt more bad for what happed to Nicky. He went into his other stashed spot were he kept 150g's at and took out 15g's and handed it to Nicky when she came out of the shower, "I'm sorry for what happened to you baby girl, this is for your trouble." Nicky took the money then told him that she wasn't going to report it to the police, but she didn't ever want to see him again. Wheel's felt bad and could do nothing but agree, as Nicky walked out the door and left.

Nicky got home and was furious. She called up her friend and her friend answer the phone on the first ring.

"Hello."

"Hello my ass nigga, why you do that to me?"

"My bad beautiful! You know that we had to make it look good, and this way you can have away out of the relationship without any suspicion." Her long time friend said with a chuckle in his voice.

Plus you know that I've wanted to hit that pussy for the longest, and I couldn't resist after seeing you in that thong.

"Your crazy! Where's my damn money? Nicky asked.

"Don't trip, I got it right here for you....you got a $40,000 thousand dollar cut, plus I'ma give you another $40g's after we finish selling this work. You're cool with that?"

"Yea that's love." Nicky said with a smile on her face.

"O'kay come by my spot and pick-up your share. Plus, put back on a thong for me.... I need to finish what I started o'kay?"

"You got that, but I'm not fuckin Sam little dick ass no more, he only lasted two minutes. He should be ashamed of himself." Nicky said as they both laughed and hung up.

Chapter 8
Never Sleep!

G-Fly just got through dropping off a hundred kilos to Princess and the girls stash house when he stopped at the fish fast food restaurant on 53rd street. He went in and ordered six red snapped plates with six side orders of fried shrimps and fried oysters. "Man that pretty lady of yours must still be pregnant?" The cook hollered out to G-Fly as he smiled.

"Naw player, this is just a after shock craving!" And they both started busting up.

"So what did you guys have?" The casher asked.

"Another boss player!"

"Here you go player, enjoy." The cooked said as he handed G-Fly his four big bags of food. "I made it fat for you and the little lady, but don't get mad at me if she gains a little weight."

"Naw, but I'm sure going to be mad at her ass!" G-Fly said as he walked out!

G-Fly jumped in his big Chevy Blazer rent a truck, and drove off.

"Ah, look ain't that one of those baller niggas?"

"Hell yea, that's one of them dead niggas there.....let's get this fool," Felony said as he rolled in the passenger set of his homeboys under cover bucket, an old 75 Monte Carlo.

The old Monte Carlo swooped out into traffic as they drove trying to catch up with the white Blazer that G-Fly was driving.

G-Fly saw the two niggas sitting in the old school Monte Carlo when he left the fast food fish restaurant, then he saw the same Monte Carlo speeding up in back of him and he smiled and rolled down his driver side window, then jumped in the right lane so he could have the advantage.

G-Fly grabbed his new baby from in the passenger seat that was hidden up under his black leather Boomer Jacket. G-Fly slowed up to miss the light and looked around for any signs of police cars around the area, then he looked in his driver side window and saw the Monte Carlo pulling up along side of him. As it got close enough, he reached out of his driver side window and started unloading the Mac 10 into the front wind shield of the Monte Carlo.

Felony was about to reach out of the passenger side window and shoot G-Fly as he sat at the stop light, but before he had an opportunity to shot, he saw an arm come out of the driver side window holding a big black box Mac 10 machine gun and fire started coming out of the barrel of the gun as Felony ducked down and heard bullets ricocheting off the hood of their car and going through the wind shield. Felony held his big 357 magnum out of his window and started bussin' at the truck while his head was still down.

G-Fly emptied his clip to his Mac 10 into the Marte Carlo then heard loud gun shots coming from the car as the side of his wind shield shattered, and he heard bullets penetrate the body of his truck. He put his head down and sped off through the red light and almost got hit by a tow truck as he flew though the intersection.

Felony heard the Mac 10 stop shooting as he started shooting back, then he heard the truck speed off and he looked up and saw the truck pulling off and yelled, "Go get that nigga," then looked over at his homeboy Banger slumped over the steering wheel drenched in blood. Felony grabbed Banger's 9mm out of his hands and aimed it out the window at the speeding truck and started unloading the 9mm at the back of the truck. The white Blazer back window shattered as it sped off down the street.

"Damn! I'ma kill all of these crazy young niggas." Felony said as he pulled Banger from the driver seat, then jumped behind the wheel and sped off.

G-Fly was laughing to himself as he pulled through the alley-way into the back yard of one of his safe houses. Then went inside and called Lady-G.

* * * *

Wheels was collecting all of his money off his dope spot so that he could use it to cop with. All was accounted for as he was about to pull out from the old lady drive-way, that he always park at when he was on the block, then he looked down the street and saw all hell break loose.

Two old cars pulled up on the block at the same time and came to a sudden stop, as three mask men jumped out of both cars and started shooting everybody that was on the block.

Wheels saw Tim-Tim get hit while sitting on the hood of a parked car and the 12 gage shot-gun blow a hole through his chest and came out of his back. Dre jumped out of the car that Tim-Tim just got shot off of, and started bussin' his 9mm at the mask man who jumped out with the 12 gage and another mask man open fired with a Uzi submachine gun and shredded Dre's body like swish cheese. Fat Rob who was behind a cement wall jump-up shooting at the mask men as Tic was on the other side of the street with C-Dog bussin' their 9mm at the mask attackers.

One of the mask men saw Fat Rob duck behind the cement wall and smiled as he unloaded his AK-47 at the area where Fat Rob ducked at, and the bullets from the big assault rifle went right through the cement wall and ate Fat Rob's body up.

Wheels jumped out of his undercover Buick and started bussin' his 45 automatic at the mask men, one got hit in the leg as both of the two mask men with AK-47 assault rifles turned on Wheels as the bullets ate up the side of his Buick and Wheels broke toward the back of the old lady's house running full speed.

Tic and C-Dog saw Wheels run and they both tried to break and run too, but C-Dog was too slow as the 12 gage and Mac 10 caught him in strive and dropped him to the ground. Tic hit the fence of the neighbors yard, and was gone through the side of the house without a scratch on him.

The mask men jumped back into their buckets and drove off. Monster was down the street in is new rent-a-car and laughed as he saw his young crew put in work. The mask men shot and killed Tim-Tim, Dre, Big Rob and six smokers and a nine year old boy, and wounded C-Dog as he laid in his own puddle of blood praying that the police will come on time to save him.

* * * *

Princess got a call from an old lady that she always paid to keep an eye on the activities that go on around that area. Princess called and told Lady-G and Lady-G walked into the work out room where G-Fly and Ty was kicking it getting high watching Julian work out.

"Baby I got some crazy news to tell you!" G-Fly and Ty looked up at her as Julian stop in a set of jumping-jacks to give Lady-G his full attention.

"Wheels dope block on the eastside low bottom just got shoot up, by some niggas with ski mask on."

"Ain't that a bitch, I told ya'll that we had to miss the niggas who's been calling the shots and trying to take us out. We must've hit his worker at the motel." G-Fly said with a serious look on is face.

"You may be right! If so, then we better warn Princess and them and try to find out who this nigga from Compton is, because he got to be really mad at the way we smashed his crew," said Ty.

"Yea, and they sure tried to catch the Fly slippin, but they got to come better then a drive-by at a red light to get at me." G-Fly said as he smiled and hit the joint.

"Did anyone get hit during the shoot-out?" Julian asked Lady-G.

"Oh yea, Miss Tee said that ten people got killed including a nine year old kid!"

"Damn that's crazy for real." Julian said as he shook his head and looked at Ty and G-Fly.

"What about Wheels? Did they get his punk ass!" G-Fly asked.

"No, lady Tee said that he was on the block when it happened and he was parked down the street from where it initially started at. She said that he jumped out of his car and shot at the attackers, and they started returning shots back at him so he ran, and that's when the nine year old boy got shot. Wheels made them shoot in his direction and the little boy was playing in back of where Wheels was parked, and when they turned their attention at Wheels the little boy got hit with a stray bullet."

"I told ya'll that we should've smoked his ass when he violated our code. Then the little boy would still be alive!" G-Fly argued his claim.

"Hold up, you can't use that to put a dent in our emotions. Just because he copped from another source don't give us the right to kill him. We quit fucking with him because of it, and now he got to deal with his own issues. Whatever happens on his dope blocks is not our business, so if they take over his spots then it's good, because it would make them easier targets for us. Right now we don't know who we're warring against, and that's our first priority. So let's focus on our ghost so we can get back to making this money. Lady-G can you please go contact Princess and let the girls know that our war is still in full swing!" Julian stated.

"Yes Boss," Lady-G said as she smiled at Julian knowing that he was back to his old self again.

"I still say that we should kill his punk ass!" G-Fly muttered as he passed Ty the joint.

After Princess got off the phone with Lady-G she got a phone call from Wheels. When Wheels left the dope spot after the shoot out, the old lady who house driveway wheels car was parked at, went outside to see the damage to her house and she was furious at the gun shots holds that was in the side of her house.

She saw Wheels car in her driveway with big holds all through the body of his car, and the windows shot out. She walked up and looked in his car and saw a purple Crown Royal clothe bag with bulges all in it. She reached into the car and grab the bag then heard the police coming, so she rushed back in side her house. When she got inside she opened up the purple bag and wads of money was filled to the top. She laughed as she heard the police stop in front of her house, so she ran and hid the money.

Wheels car got towed away so Wheels believed that the police must've confiscated his money.

"Come on Princess this is me, your boy! I really need some work!" Wheels said as he tried to beg Princess to sell him something.

"I've already told you Wheels, we're not doing nothing right now!" Princess said as she looked over at Little Tish and rolled her eyes in an irritated manner.

"Well listen, just let me hold around 30g's then!" Wheels asked.

"You're crazy if you think that I'ma give you my money....What happen to your money?"

"It's a long story!"

"Well I got some extra time," said Princess.

"I got jacked!"

"What, I didn't catch that."

"I said, I got jacked a while back and they got me for a grip!" Wheels said in a low voice.

"What's a grip?" Princess asked as she smiled at Little Tish who was trying to make out what Princess was talking about.

"They got me for 230g's and seven keys." Wheels said in a disappointed manner.

"Damn, that had to hurt! How they catch you slippin like that?" Princess asked as Little Tish eyes got big and they both laughed silently.

"That don't make no damn difference, either your gonna let me borrow the money or not!" Wheels scream through the phone in an agitated voice.

"What a minute nigga, you called me asking me for a fuckin favor, and you think that I'ma let you just talk to me anyway. You got to be crazy! As a matter of fact, you can loose my muthafucken number, because were all through fuckin with your dumb ass.

You choose to go outside the family and find friends, and I suggest that you continue to do so!" Princess hung up the phone in his face as she and Little Tish started bustin up and gave each other a high five.

"That nigga just said that he got jacked for 230g's and seven keys. Princess told Little Tish as they sat in a booth at a Mexican restaurant.

"You're bullshitting girl!" Little Tish muttered as she put her small hand over her mouth. What happened?"

"He wouldn't tell me, he got all mannish on the phone and I had to check his punk ass!"

"About time...! I hate to wish bad luck on a nigga, but that's what his stupid ass gets for going outside of the family and getting work. That's that greed catching up to him!" Little Tish said. Princess just started laughing as she shook her head yes!

Two nigga in their twenties was on the other side of the restaurant glancing over at Princess and Little Tish and they finally got the nerves to walk over and introduce themselves.

"Hello ladies, how are ya'll doing today?" The light skinned one with wavy hair asked.

"We're fine..." Princess answered with a friendly smile.

"Me and my man couldn't help but notice both of you beautiful ladies from across the room, and being that we're from different cities, we were hoping that you ladies could show us around and allow us the privilege of wining and dining you."

Princess and Little Tish was really uninterested but Princess didn't want to be rude, so she asked, "so where did you say that you were from?"

"Oh, we're from Compton! We're just out here thinking about investing in a clothing store, so were looking around and seeing if we can find a nice location." The light skinned one said. "My name is Shawn, and this is my homeboy Troy." Troy was a dark skin, tall pretty boy with short waves going through his hair.

"Please to meet you," Princess said with a smile. My name is Toy, and this is my friend Candy! We work at a strip club in Pasadena. Each time I visit my sister, I have to stop in here and grab me a couple of their taco's and burrito special." Little Tish just sat there with a cute smile on her face, playing along with Princess little game because she already knew what Princess was up to.

"Oh yea, that's what's up! Me and my man would like to hire you both for a private party." Shawn said as he knew that they just came up on some quick and easy pussy.

"Well, if you got time, then me and my girl can give ya'll a little private party now. We're booked later though!"

"Yea we got the time!" Shawn said with a lustful grin.

"Well give us a hundred dollars a piece and go get a motel room down the street at the Travel Lodge so we can kick it there." Princess said with a flirtatious smile.

"That's what's up, let's go! Don't worry I got the bill." Shawn looked at Troy as Princess and Little Tish got up from the table and their bodies were like that. They followed the girls out of the restaurant as Princess and Little Tish big butt hypnotized them every step of the way.

Princess and Little Tish jumped in their new Nissan Maximum rent a car and lead the way to the motel. Princess said, "stay on point Tish, we're going to draw down on these niggas and hold them until Ty and them come, and hopefully we can get some information out of them. Call the main house and tell them where we going.

Tish jumped on her cell phone and called the main house and Julian answered the phone.

"Hello?"

"Hey J., this is Lil momma, me and Ms P, got some hustlers from C Town that we're taking to the Travel Lodge Motel on Western! Hold on! (Tish said as she put the phone down then asked, what room did you get? Room 69....! O'kay we'll park over there) "O'kay J. we're in room 69, we'll hold them until ya'll get here, bye...."

Julian hung up the phone then called Big Bro. After telling Big Bro what was up and where to meet them, he ran in the other room and told Lady-G. Then ran to the gun closet and grabbed a 9mm with a silencer, some hand cuffs and a bullet proof vest just in case. He ran down stairs and Lady-G was waiting for him. "Where do you think your going?"

"I'm going with you!" Lady-G said with a where you think look on her face.

"No you're not," Julian order.

"Listen I'm grown Julian and believe me, I've been doing this shit way before you." Lady-G looked at him with a sarcastic look on her face.

Julian knew that she was right so he said, "Listen Lady-G, I know that you're the downest woman that we got, but I need you to play your part, not mine! Let me play my role and you play yours. I need you

116

to watch over our empire in case we get knocked, then we know that we have someone on point who's gonna make sure that our business gets handle. So know that your position is very valuable to us." Lady-G stuck out her lips like a little girl, then Julian kissed her on her forehead and said, "do you feel me?" She smiled and shook her head as Julian ran out the door and was gone.

* * * *

Princess and Little Tish walked into the motel room in back of the guys as they were contemplating their next move.

Shawn went over and cut on the light as Troy went over to the TV and cut on the radio and when they turned around to look at the girls, Princess had her 3.80 pointed at Shawn and Lil Tish had her new 357 snub nose revolver pointed at Troy. "Oh shit," Troy said as he tried to block the bullet with his hands.

"What the fuck?" Shawn said.

"Get on the ground nigga, and put your hands on your muthafucken head, you know the damn position!" Tish said as they both laughed.

"O'kay…. Don't shoot!"

"Nigga I will light your big ass up if you try something slick….you better hurry up!" Troy and Shawn fell to the ground. Tish looked over at Princess and said "search them."

Princess went over to Shawn and took his 45 automatic from the side of his waist band, and put the gun on safety as she dropped the clip and ejected the extra bullet in the chamber, then sat the gun on the table. She then went over to Troy and took a 9mm out of his waist band, and dropped the clip and ejected the bullets as she laid it next to the other gun.

"Who are you bitches?" Troy asked as he glanced up at Little Tish from the floor.

"We are two police bitches that will kill you if you think about trying us." Tish said as Princess looked over at her like 'bitch, I know that you didn't just say that we were some police'. Tish saw the look in Princess eyes and shrugged her shoulders.

"We ain't did nothing wrong!" Troy argued.

"Oh yea, do you have a license to carry these guns?" Tish asked in her defense.

"No...! But I know my rights, and this is an illegal search!" Troy added.

"Not really, see we're investigating a string of homicides that's been taking place around here. A lot of innocent women has been lured to motels around here and brutally raped and killed."

"We ain't raped and killed nobody. I know my rights and you ain't got no right holding us at gun point like this." Shawn said in a hostile voice.

Princess grabbed his empty big 45 automatic off the table and walked over to him and stood over him, and when he looked up at her, she started slapping him in the head with the gun. She hit him five good times and then went back over to the table and sat down as the blood ran down Shawn head and face.

"See you've pissed my partner off, and as you can see, we're not here to play no games with you!" Tish said as she laughed and they heard a knock at the door. Princess got up to answer it and looked out the window and saw that it was Big Bro and opened up the door.

"Damn, what took you so long? I thought that I might have to catch a hot one-on-one of these sucka." Princess said as she closed the door.

Troy said, "they ain't no damn police," and jumped to his feet as Little Tish lifted her gun about to shoot, and saw Big Bro kick Troy in the nuts, then kneed him in the face busting his nose as Troy fell back against the wall, and then Big Bro kicked the side of Troy's leg breaking it on contact as Troy fell back onto the floor.

"Damn he fucked him up!" Little Tish said then turned toward Shawn and said, "Your ass is next if you try anything slick." She looked over at Princess and started laughing. Just then they heard another knock at the door and Princess walked over to answer it, as Julian walked in.

"What's up baby," Julian said as he kissed Princess on the lips then bent down and kissed Tish on the lips and smiled at Big Bro when he saw the man laying in the corner with a busted nose, holding his broken leg. Julian smiled and asked, "Is that your work or Princesses?"

"That's his work over there and that's mine!" Princess said as she pointed to the other light skinned nigga who's head and face was bloody.

Julian laughed then went over and hand cuffed Shawn, then went over and did the same to Troy. "Who the fuck is ya'll and what do you want from us?"

"Well, we're the ones who you were sent to come out here and kill! Either you tell us what we need to know, or we're going to torture you and then kill you. Or you could tell us and we'll let you go, but if you ever come back to our city again then I'll kill you on sight!"

"How do we know that you won't just kill us anyway?" Shawn said in a whinnying voice.

"What choice do you have?" Julian asked as he seat down in a chair next to where Shawn was laying.

"Don't tell his bitch ass nothing," Troy said from across the room as Big Bro walked over to him and stuck him in the eye with his big Rambo knife and Troy was dead before Big Bro even pulled it back out.

"Damn, that shit was straight nasty! Cover his ass up and put him in the closet! I don't wannabe looking at his one eye ass to long." Princess said as she squinted her face. Little Tish laughed as Big Bro took the quilt off the bed and throw it over the body and drugged it into the closet." That's better; now what was you telling this fool daddy?"

"Oh yeah, it's up to you, either you can end up like your friend, or you can be the smart one and leave here alive. It's your choice!" Julian said as he lifted Shawn's big bloody 45 automatic from the table and looked at it, then at Princess, as she shrugged her shoulders and smiled.

"O'kay man, I ain't trying to die like this! What do you want to know? Shawn said as the thought of dying changed his mind.

"Who is Little Creep, Monster, and Felony? Julian asked.

Shawn's eyes got big at the mention of Little Creep and Monsters name. He smiled and said, "It looks like you've been doing your homework!"

Julian said, "Let's just say that someone was smart enough to live, instead of die!"

Shawn's eyes deemed as he was contemplating his move, then he said "Little Creep is a kingpin out of Compton who wants to take over Los Angeles territory. Some big kingpin died a while ago, and his young crew, which I imagine is you, took over his territory and Little Creep wants to take it from you. Monster is his enforcer and gives the orders, and Felony is more like the Lieutenant that they sent out here to set up shop and take you guys out. But it seem as though you guys are tougher then they anticipated, so Little Creep sent Monster out here to help handle the take over, cause you guys were a little to tough for Felony and Crime, 'rest in peace'."

"How do this Little Creep, Monster, and Felony look?" Julian asked.

Well Little Creep is about 5'7" and 165 lbs with a baby face, but is heartless. Monster on the other hand is 6'5" and 285 lbs with a muscular built, brown skin and big crazy droopy eyes. Felony is a big fat black nigga who likes to wear a lot of jewelry."

"That's the one that we tried to kill at the red light." Tish said to Princess so they knew that Shawn was telling the truth so far.

"Oh, that was ya'll....! He said that it was two crazy young bitches who tried to get at him. Damn! I should've listened to him."

"Where do they live?"

"Well, no one really knows where Little Creep lives at; he's to smart for that. You'll have to catch Felony or Monster slippin for that information, and good luck on that! Shawn said as he started laughing then looked backup and saw that no one else was laughing with him so he said, "I don't know where Monster lives at either, he's like a fuckin ghost! He'll pop up when you lease expect it, and you'll be spooked. But Felony, I've been to his house once since I've been out here, and he has a house that he's renting on 53rd and 4th Ave. I don't know his address or nothing, but I know that's his street because he gave me direction when I went over there."

"O'kay, but where do all ya'll stay at?"

"He got us a house off of Slauson in back of the Slauson Swap Meet, It's a big yellow house with an old wooden fence around it. I can show you if you want. Just let me roll out and you guys won't ever see me again. This ain't my war, and I'm cool on all this crazy shit. I got a pregnant wife and two kids at home and I just want to be there for them." Shawn expressed as Julian eyes got dark with hatred and envy, as Shawn mentioned his pregnant wife and kids.

He looked up at Big Bro and said, "One thing that I really hate is a nigga who would betray and snitch on his friends... kill this pathetic son-of-a-bitch!"

Big Bro smiled and said, "With pleasure," as he started walking toward Shawn. Shawn hollered out, "Wait man why you trippin?" Then he tried to scream as Big Bro kicked him in the mouth with his steal toe boots and broke Shawn's jaw, then reached down and grabbed him by the head and face and twisted it in two separate directions, and instantly popped his neck.

"Damn, now that was some gangsta shit there!" Princess said as her and Tish smiled at each other then shook to shake the eerie feeling from their bones.

"I know that daddy was about to smash his ass. He had that crazy look in his eyes like Jack Nicholson in the Shinning." Tish said as everyone started laughing and Julian just shook his head.

"Listen, I want ya'll to go grab some towels out of the bathroom and wet them, and start wiping down everything in here that ya'll think that we could've touched." Julian ordered.

"O'kay baby!" Princess and Tish said as they got up and went to grab some towels.

"Those got to be some of the downest ladies in the world." Big Bro said as he looked at Julian.

"Yea, and they got some sisters just as crazy and down as they are."

"Hey J, before I forget, I talked to sergeant and she's interested in coming aboard." Big Bro said.

"She?" Julian asked as he lifted his eye brows.

"Yep, and I'm sure that she'll fit right in with the other crazy ladies around here. Picture them two right there with expert combat skills." Big Bro made reference to Princess and Little Tish.

"Is that right?" Big Bro shook his head yes.

"Well bring her by the house this evening and we'll check her out. Also, we got some planning to do," and they both started smiling in agreement.

Chapter 9
Ghetto War Games

It was six o'clock in the evening as Julian, Ty, G-Fly, Lady-G, Princess, Dee-Dee, Gwen, and Little Tish was all in the dining room at the round table discussing their plan to hit the Compton niggas kicked spot. Julian and Big Bro already pasted by the location and saw a couple of niggas hanging out on the porch and a few cars parked in the drive-way. So they were sure that was the spot that, that nigga Shawn was talking about. If not, then oh well, the game had gotten to crucial to second guess their enemies position.

"Listen I say that we just run in there and smoke everything in the house." G-Fly firmly said.

"Why not set the house on fire and kill niggas as they run out." Dee-Dee said tapping into her treacherous ways.

"That's way too crazy because a lot of innocent people can get hurt by it. What if the fire blows out of control and kill innocent families. That will put us in the category of some cold hearted killer, and that's not what we our. We protect what's ours, and kill anyone who opposes it or get in the way!" Julian said.

"Yea, similar to the United States!" G-Fly said as everyone shared a good laugh.

"Listen, I kinda' like G-Fly method," Ty said. "I think that we should creep on these niggas at night, and go in poppin everything in there. We can creep with the silencers on the guns and if we do it right, then we can creep back out without alerting the neighbors."

"Yea I'm down with however ya'll want to do it! Princess said.

"Good because we need ya'll to be on point outside in the cars, so ya'll can be our get away drivers if things get out of control," said Ty.

"I don't want to drive. I want to bust my gun too," Little Tish said as she gave Dee-Dee a high five.

"Listen we all appreciate the way you bitches been holding this family down and we know that ya'll are ready to die for the cause, but ya'll better learn how to take orders and except the position that we need ya'll to play. If we need ya'll to go in there bussin' your guns, then we're going to ask ya'll to do so, but if we need ya'll to drive the get away cars, then bitch that's gonna be your muthafucken job! Now is it anyone here who can't relate to this? G-Fly strongly emphasized. All of the girls at the table looked around and then looked at G-Fly.

Princess said, "We feel you daddy and we're down for whatever!"

"Good...! Now this is the way that I feel we should attack this situation." And G-Fly started giving everybody the run down.

After they finished putting the plan together they heard a knock at the door, which was to the beat of their secret knock. G-Fly thought of it and taught it to Cindy, just in case someone got in and had Cindy at gun point, then she would just give a regular type knock, then open up the door and fall to the ground, as everybody else would be on point and start shooting at the intruders. Cindy always got a kick out of the youngsters' humor and extreme thoughts, but she knew better then to question them. "Come in!" G-Fly said.

As Cindy peeped in and said, "Mr. Big Bro and his friend has arrived."

"Good, take them into the living room we'll be right there," Julian said as Ty and G-Fly looked at him confused. Julian looked at Lady-G and said, "Make sure that ya'll have your game down."

"O'kay." Lady-G said.

"G-Fly, Ty…. Come with me for a minute." Julian said as Ty and G-Fly excused themselves from the table and followed Julian out the door.

They walked in the living-room and Big Bro was sitting on the couch with a cute Puerto Rican lady. "Hey little bro's, I like you to meet my best friend in the whole wide world, this is my Sergeant Evelyn….Evelyn this is my three younger brothers."

"Hi, please to meet you, Kevin speaks very highly of you!" Evelyn said.

"Hold up, this is Sergeant? Ty asked.

"Yes that's her." Big Bro said with a smile.

"Is there a problem?" Evelyn said as she looked at Ty crazy as Ty walked around her in a complete 360 degree circle, checking her out from head to toe.

"Well I'm really kind of surprised. I was expecting a male version of the sergeant, not the female version." Ty admitted.

"So what skills do you have?" G-Fly asked.

"I'm a sharp shooter, and I specialize in different degrees of hand to hand combat and I specialize also in high technology investigation, and….

"Hold up!" Ty said interrupting Evelyn in the middle of her resume' speech. "You can't be no threat to anyone! You're only 5'2" and around 115 lbs tops how can you stop a man that's over 200 lbs and standing 6 feet or better? She's lying!"

"Evelyn honey coated complexion instantly became a reddish tint, as she looked at Big Bro and Big Bro shrugged his shoulder and she looked at Ty and said, "You're around 190 lbs and I say about 5'10", maybe you'll like to see for yourself?"

"Ooowww, no she didn't go there." Julian said instigating the issue.

"I don't normally waste my time putting my hands on a woman, but don't tempt me." Ty said as he smiled at Julian and G-Fly.

"Yea right! That's just a cop out…. your just scared that you might get your ass whooped." Evelyn said.

As Julian, G-Fly and Big Bro started wooing and laughing real hard. G-Fly said, "I like this bitch she got heart."

"Yea a little to much heart to be talking shit to me like that… I should kick her little fine ass just for fun." Ty said as he laughed with G-Fly and Julian.

"Yea right nigga, you're all bark with no bite!" Evelyn said as she looked Ty up and down.

"O'kay bitch, let's see how tough you really are," and Ty put his hands up and shot a quick jab at Evelyn that she seen coming a mile away and side stepped it, then hit Ty in the mouth with a open hand palm then spun around and kicked Ty in the stomach with a round house that seat him on the ground and knocked the wind out of him.

Lady-G and the girls was walking up when they saw Ty fly back and hit the ground. G-Fly said, "Damn babe fucked you up!" Then he saw Lady-G and the girls walk up and said, "ya'll just in time to see Ty get his ass whooped." And him, Julian and Big Bro started busting up.

Ty got up and said, "that was pretty good, but I see that I ain't got to take it easy on you", then he tried to rush her with a quick three piece combination and she blocked them with ease as she caught the last punch and went down on one knee and socked Ty in the lower stomach, then stood up as Ty arched over from the blow and tripped him over her leg as she watched him fall to the ground, but rolled all the way over his head and shoulder and back onto is feet, as he rushed her trying to grab hold of her upper body and she went down with the momentum and used his body force as she rolled on her back and kicked his body over hers, as he landed over her head on his back and she was on top of him sitting on his chest with her small fist balled up and aimed at his face. He opened up his eyes and smiled and said, "O'kay you got the job!"

Everyone started clapping as Evelyn got up and gave Ty a hand up. Big Bro said, "You're lucky that she took it easy on you! She's the one who trained me in a lot of the Martial Arts."

Everyone looked at Evelyn with a different perspective. "O'kay now that we got that question out the way. Tell me Evelyn, do you know what you're getting involved in?" Julian asked as everyone stood around in the living room gazing at one another.

"Yes I believe so!"

"Well let me be more frank with you! If you chose to come into this family then you become a part of us for life. We live by a very strict type of ghetto codes and ethic that could never be compromised or broken for any reason. We will give our life for one another, as well as kill to protect one another with our last breath. Anyone who opposes us is a threat and that includes police, judges, prosecutors, and politicians. No one is exempt when it comes to our family and the love, honor, protection, and loyalty that we give to it. Now, the consequence of being a part of our family is prison or death! That's why we live by the morals and laws that we've established to protect our family, and one of the primary laws is silence and secrecy! Our business is nobody else's business, and as long as you honor this law in your heart, then you could never betray your family or hurt us. Do you understand this law?"

"Yes I do."

"Do you honestly believe that you can live by it, kill by it, and die by it? And what I mean by kill by it is,....if Big Bro should violate this law and say something that could jeopardize this family, then your obligated to kill him and visa versa! Do you believe that you can live by this, and the other things that I have expressed?"

"Yes I could and I will."

Julian looked over at G-Fly and Ty and G-Fly said, "Do you know that we're caught up in a war against other gangsta who's trying to kill us, and we got to get them first to survive."

"Yes sir, I understand that my job will consist of killing anyone who opposes us."

"She's smart, I like her! Ty said with a smile on his face.

"Well it looks like she understands what's going on and what's required of her." Julian said.

"Wait, do you understand that us three sit at the head of this family and our word is law here." G-Fly asked.

"Yes sir, Kevin mentioned that there are three Generals that sit at the head of the table, and that you three are as real and down as they come, he also said that there was a queen in the family as well." Evelyn said with a smile as she looked around at the ladies.

"Well I'm glad that you were well informed! This is the Lady-G the appointed queen of the family, and these lovely ladies is our beautiful wives and gangsta bitches! This is Princess, that's Dee-Dee, her over there is Gwen, and this is Little Tish. Ladies this is Big Bro Sergeant AKA Lil Momma. And everyone laughed at Evelyn's new nick name that G-Fly just gave her.

"Lil Momma! That ain't my nick name."

"It is now girl," Princess said and everyone laughed as Evelyn made a mean face at G-Fly then started laughing too.

"Well I guess that that makes it official then! Put it in the Air!!! Ty said.

"I'll smoke to that," G-Fly said then looked at Lady-G and said, "How about grabbing some drinks I'll take some Louise the XIII myself," and smiled.

"I got you baby," Lady-G said as she gave him a kiss and walked away.

Listen Lil Momma, we're going to set you up with a nice place to live, and get you a car and some fly gear, because you're a part of us and that's how we live. You'll work with Big Bro at the Private Eye Service that we established for him, and we'll start you off at $100g's a year for your work with us and put you on a salary with the security service so you can account for your life style. Don't worry, we're going to make sure that you have the best, just always keep it real with us, and watch our backs like we will always watch yours." Julian expressed as Ty seat on the other side of her shaking his head in agreement and smoking a joint with G-Fly and Big Bro.

* * * *

It was the following night and the plan called, "The extermination," was in full effect. It was 10:30p.m. and the neighborhood was starting to quiet down. Ty and Julian were approaching the back way through the house that was on the back street, with the back yard connected to the Compton niggas back yard. Ty gazed into the window of the old house that they had to walk by to get to the Compton niggas back gate, and he seen an old man sitting in front of his TV watching a movie. Ty motioned to Julian as they proceeded to walk by the windows of the old man's house bent down low. They made it to the back cement 8 feet wall and pulled their guns out. Julian had a 9mm with a silencer and a 357 magnum in a hoster as his back up, and Ty had a 45 automatic with a silencer and a Mac 10 Uzi on a purse strap hanging from his shoulder. They looked over the gate and didn't see anything, so they jumped up and over the gate then Julian saw a big black shadow running toward them and he raised his gun and shot three times at the figure as the big black pit bull fell five feet away from them.

"Damn that was close." Ty muttered.

Julian grabbed his walkie-talkie and said "were home and about to lay down!"

"Got-cha." G-Fly said into his walkie-talkie receiver as him and Big Bro existed the G-ride and walked up toward the front door of the Compton niggas low key spot.

When Julian shot the dog, one of the bullets went stray and hit the side of the house. Slim was in the kitchen when he heard the noise and he thought that it was Blacky, Devil's black pit bull. Slim opened the back door and looked out into the back yard and called Blacky, then he seen two figures and heard two shots fire, then he felt his chest burning as he fell on the ground. Ty and Julian ran into the kitchen and Ty shot Slim one more time in the head as they ran in. Julian picked up his walker-talkie and said, "We're in."

Spider and Mouse was in the living room watching 48 Hours with Eddie Murphy in it. When Spider heard a hard thump on the ground coming from the kitchen, and he got up from the couch and went to go see what it was. As he approached the kitchen he saw two male figures with ski masks on standing over Slims body as Slim laid on the ground in a puddle of blood. Spider reached for his 44 magnum and felt bullets penetrate his body multiple times as his body flew back into the living room and landed on the floor. Mouse jumped up in shock as the front door got kicked in and someone rolled onto the living room floor then came up from the roll bussin', hitting him twice in the heart and once in the forehead. G-Fly was right in back of him with his gun raised and pointed around the room. G-Fly looked toward the stairs and Big Bro lead the way as G-Fly and Ty followed him and Julian stayed down stairs moving the bodies and making sure nobody came in while their backs was turned.

Big Bro, G-Fly and Ty hit each room one at a time. They heard some moaning coming from one of the rooms and Ty held up his hand to stop everyone, as he slowly turned the knob and opened up the door, then they all walked in with their guns drawn and saw this fat light skin nigga on top of this ugly dark skin girl fuckin her hard and fast. She opened her eyes and instantly froze up when she saw the three figures dressed in black with ski masks on staring at her. Devil the big fat light skin nigga looked at the smoker bitch that he was fuckin and wonder why she stopped humping back, and he saw her eyes bucked so he eased his hand under the pillow and turned around as he tried to bring his 9mm up, and felt lighting shoot all through his body as Big Bro, Ty and G-Fly all unloaded three shots a piece in his fat 300 pound body.

"OH shit, Oh shit!" The smoker bitch yelled as Big Bro socked her in the jaw and knocked her out cold. Then he removed the 9mm from the fat light skin dude's hand.

Two cars pulled up in front of the Compton niggas low key spot and princess and Little Tish was parked at one end of the corner and Dee-Dee and Gwen was at the other end. Princess looked over at Little Tish and said, "We got company." Then she smiled over at Little Tish and cocked her 9mm as Little Tish smiled and took her Big 45 automatic off safety. "We better create a diversion for them. I'll drive you bust!"

"Whatever you say," Tish said as she grabbed princess 9mm and rolled down her window.

Two niggas got out of the 5.0 sitting on Dayton wire rims, and three more got out of the black Chevy Blazer sitting on triple gold Dayton wire rims. They were walking up toward the walkway to the house as a 82 Cutless pulled up and started bussin' shot at them. JR and Poe-Poe both dove on the ground and pulled their guns out and started bussin' back as their other three homeboy was layed face down on the ground and the Cutless sped-off burning rubber.

"Ain't that a bitch cuz! Shit they smoke the homies," JR said to Poe-Poe as they looked down at their homeboys face down twisted in a puddle of blood. The front door to the house opened up and a hail of silent bullets rained on JR and Poe-Poe as their bodies was riddled with bullets holes.

"Let's roll," Julian said, then turned toward G-Fly and said, "Ya'll meet us at the spot," and Julian and Ty ran back through the back door, the same way they came. G-Fly and Big Bro ran and jumped in their G-ride and peeled out as Dee-Dee and Gwen pulled out in front of them, and went through the alley where G-Fly and Big Bro burned their car, then jumped in the car with Dee-Dee and Gwen, and they drove off to meet up at the safe house.

Julian and Ty ran and jumped in the back seat of Lady-G rent a car and she pulled off headed for the safe house. Julian looked over at Ty and said, "What the hell happened back there?"

"I don't know, Maybe a rival gang decided to get at them, and caught them slippin as they got out of their cars." Ty reasoned.

"No telling, but I know they laid down three of them before we got at the other two." Julian said as he pondered over the incident. Lady-G pulled up in the driveway of the safe house, and they all got out and walked into the house.

Everybody already made it to the house and was smoking weed and sippin alcohol. "What's up my nigga? I love it when a good plan comes together. G-Fly said as he gave his comrades a ghetto embrace.

Julian smiled and said, "Yea, I love a good plan too, but what happen to them other niggas that was shot dead in the front yard before we opened up the door and got at the other two?"

"Man you don't know? That was your two crazy ass ghetto wives work! They saw them nigga pull up while we was in the house and decided to create a diversion, and did an old fashion style drive-by to give us time to gain the upper hand," G-Fly said as he had his arm around Princesses neck and kissed her on the cheek.

Julian and Ty smiled as they held out their arms and gave Princess and Little Tish a big hug.

"Listen I'ma shower then me, Lady-G and Princess is going to go get rid of these guns at the pier, then go home and enjoy some quality time," said G-Fly.

"O'kay, I'ma take Big Bro to the Mansion in Altadena and let him enjoy some of the best pussy in the world. Julian said as the three youngsters looked at Big Bro from across the room talking to Lady-G and started laughing.

"What about you Ty, what are you about to do?" G-Fly asked.

"I'ma go kick it with Dee-Dee, Gwen, and Little Tish….they deserve to get some tonight," Ty said as he smiled.

"Yea, we got to do something special for them after we finish getting shit back in order," Julian said.

"I can have Lady-G get them some round trip tickets to Jamaica!"

"Yeah, that would be right on time! Shit we all should go!" Julian suggested.

"Yeah, I'm feeling that too! We need to hurry up and put an end to this shit before we get caught slippin on one of ours." G-Fly said.

"O'kay, we'll hit Felony in a couple of days. Tell Big Bro to sit on him so we could make sure that we hit him right. He got to be pretty paranoid now, so we don't want to make any mistakes or under estimate him."

"Sounds good to me."

"Me too," the youngsters agreed and gave each other a ghetto hand shake before they ended their pow-wow.

Chapter 10
What Is Ghetto Love and Devotion?

It was the following day and Felony was in Compton talking to Monster about the hit on the low key spot that their homies was killed at.

"I'm telling you Monster, that was those youngsters who did that! Ain't no rival gang ever put down no hit like that….they went through the house and slaughtered everybody, and the niggas down the street said they only heard someone do a drive by on the spot, but how did everybody in the house get killed?" Felony said as he tried to figure the situation out.

"Didn't the police report that you got from our inside connection say that Devil was butt naked in the bed with pussy juices on him?"

"Yep! Do you think that it was one of the same bitches that hit the motel?" Felony asked in a paranoid tone, knowing that he's scared to even meet a new bitch now, because he don't know how many crazy bitches that those youngsters may have on their team.

"Quit acting paranoid nigga,….you know how much Devil like fuckin base head bitches. He probably had one with him when this shit went down. So go check around that hood and see if you could find that bitch."

"O'kay, I'm on it! Also, there's this nigga who said that he runs the east side low bottom and he's trying to buy some work. But I don't know who this nigga is, or if he could be trusted. He might be hooked up with them youngsters," Felony said.

"Why do you think that," Monster asked?

"Because those youngsters run that area, and for him to be coppin 10 keys then he has to be fuckin with somebody. Ain't nobody stupid enough to be moving that kind of weight in someone else's territory without raising some eye brows."

"You maybe right, but he might also be the nigga we need to gain access into sellin up that part of town. Set up an appointment. I want to meet him and see if he can be useful to us."

"O'kay, I'll set it up for later on today. But do you want me to get some more low key spots so you can send some other homies."

"Shit, it seems like these young niggas got the homies spooked! Everybody that we've sent down there came back in a body bag except you. I'm starting to wonder if you're down with us or them!" Monster said as he looked Felony in the eyes.

"Ah man, I would never betray my homies like that! Felony said in a serious tone.

"I know, I just wanted to get an impulse out of you. But nigga you better put in some work! The boss was talking about how he was going to let you have power over the L.A. territory once we take it, but if you can't get the job done, then someone else is gonna end up stealing your shin." Monster said as he laughed.

"Don't worry, I got this! But these young niggas is tougher then I thought, and they're cold killers! So we got to creep and catch these niggas slippin then smash them. All that ghetto gorilla warfare shit isn't working. They seem to know all about them tactics, so we got to be more subtle and invisible." Then they smiled as Felony stood up from Monster kitchen table and gave him a ghetto hand shake and left.

Monster sat back down and contemplated his moves, then jumped on the phone and called Little Creep.

* * * *

G-Fly took Lady-G and the baby and Princess out shopping in Beverly Hills. He loved to spoil his ladies and considering that he was a young ghetto millionaire, money wasn't a thang. They sold around 200 keys a week making twelve thousand off every kilo, making a $2,400,000 dollar profit a week. After splitting it up three ways he pocket around $800,000 thousand dollars not including all of his other legitimate business venture. So all and all, G-Fly was ballin out of control and wasn't planning on relinquishing his thrown.

"More champagne Sir?" the pretty young thick blond hair lady asked.

"Why not!" G-Fly said as he held up his champagne glass to receive the bubbly as little G laid next to him sleeping in a baby carrier set.

"How do you like this daddy?" Lady-G said as she showed off her new thick figure in the two thousand dollar evening dress.

"I like it, and especially the way that it shows off that sexy fat ass of yours." Lady-G blushed then turned and looked at her backside in the large mirror.

"I'll take the black one and the red one!" Lady-G said as the cute white sales lady smiled.

Princess walked out next in a sexy low cut evening dress that was showing every part of her sexy well developed body off, and leaving nothing to the imagination. "How do you like this one daddy?"

"They should pay you to wear it, because you're killing the game with that one!" Princess smiled as she lent over and gave G-Fly a passionate kiss. Damn

baby, quit that! You're making me feel like a trick."
G-Fly said as everyone started laughing.

"I'm glad little G's asleep, he'll probably start
crying if he saw me tricking like this." And he started
shaking his head as Princess and Lady-G laughed and
walked back into the dressing room to go try on some
more clothes.

* * * *

Little Tish, Dee-Dee, and Gwen was all business
as they were running back and forth to the stash spot
getting kilos and taking money. Dee-Dee just took 30
kilos to one of their clients in Pomona, and Gwen just
took Killa 25 kilos, as Little Tish and Ty was at the
stash house counting the money that already been
made.

"I got $180,000 thousand dollars over here," Little
Tish said.

"O'kay, put it in the bag with the other 300g's that
will be $480,000 thousand dollars so far, not including
the $360,000 thousand dollars that Dee-Dee is
bringing back and the $300,000 thousand dollars that
Gwen went to get."

Tish got a page and said, "OH, this is Jay from
Pasadena, he's going to want at less 25 of them."

"How many do we have left," Ty asked?

"Gwen just took the last 25 to Killa."

"O'kay, I'ma go take this money that we already
made and put it up, and I'ma bring back a hundred
more for ya'll."

"O'kay, I'll put Jay on hold until later. Tish said
as Ty grabbed the big black duffle bag and gave her a
kiss then walked out the door.

As Ty opened up the door he felt a hard object
strike him in the face and he feel back onto the floor
of the apartment as he tried to shake the dizziness off.

Tish seen Ty fall back into the apartment and before
she could react two nigga's walked in with ski masks
on. She looked over at her purse where her big 45
automatic was in, and knew that she couldn't get to it.
"What the fuck do ya'll want?" Tish asked, as she
held her hands up.

"Shut up bitch, and get your little funky ass on
the ground," one of the mask men said as Tish layed
down right next to Ty and the other mask man
reached down and took Ty's 9mm and the big black
duffle bag off his shoulder.

Ty looked up though blurred eyes and said, "Go
on and take it, but just don't hurt us!"

"Shut up punk," the second mask man said as he
started socking Ty in the face.

"Stop it," Little Tish said as she pushed the mask
man who was socking Ty in the face, and he kicked
her in the face knocking her back to the floor as she
grabbed her eye. Then he started kicking Ty in the
face and body.

"Come on cuz, quit playing with that nigga. We
got the money already!"

"Fuck that shit cuz, tell me, where is the
muthafucken dope at nigga?" The mask man who
was whooping on Ty asked.

"We sold out, he was about to go recop now with
the money that's in the fuckin bag," Little Tish yelled.

The mask man looked at his partner then at Tish
and said, "How much money is this bitch?"

"It's around five hundred thousand dollars, take
it, and just leave us alone. You caught us slippin and
came up, now take the damn money and leave," Tish
said.

"Shut up bitch!"

"Come on man let's roll, we got the money."

"O'kay, we out but first," he aimed the gun at Ty's chest and Little Tish dove over him to try to shield him from the bullet, and the mask man looked at his partner with surprise and aimed his 9mm at Little Tish big butt, and shot her in the ass, as she screamed in pain, and the mask men laughed and walked out the door. Little Tish crawled over to her purse and grabbed her big 45 automatic. Then went over and started gently slapping Ty in the face trying to wake him up. Ty eyes started opening through the swollenness, as he saw Little Tish crying over him.

"Damn what happened baby? Are you all right?"

"No they shot me!"

"They shot you? Ty started to fight his weakness and stood up straight as he grabbed his side. Where did they shoot you at?"

"I think in the butt, my whole ass is numb."

"Let me see!" Little Tish turned around and her butt and leg was soaked in blood.

"Damn baby, don't' worry I got you!" Ty got up and staggered to the restroom were he put some cold water on his face and looked in the mirror and saw his whole facial appearance swollen. He shook his head then grabbed a big towel and walked back out with a lot more strength and control in his walk. He folded the towel up and pulled off Little Tish sweat pants and saw were the gun shot wound was and put the towel on it and said, "Hold this and put as much pressure as you can."

"Is it bad?"

"Not really, but you should be glad that you got a lot of ass!" Ty said as he smiled at her and she broke a weak smile. Ty reached down and put the 45 automatic in his waist band, then lend down and picked Little Tish up as he gritted his teeth through his own physical pain. Little Tish was little and petite so Ty was able to carry her with little effort. He carried her outside to his car and Gwen just pulled up as Ty was walking out with Tish in his arms.

Gwen jumped out of the car and said, "What happened?"

"Open up the door!" Ty said as Gwen opened up the passenger side door and Ty seat down with Little Tish in his lap and shut the door, as Gwen ran around to the driver side of the car and punched out on her way to the nearest hospital.

"What happened ya'll?"

"Someone jacked the spot, but I don't remember much," Ty said.

As they looked down at Little Tish and she started explaining what happened, and when she finished Ty was in a semi-daze as he heard how his little ghetto queen sacrificed her life to save his. He looked down at her and she just smiled and kissed him on his swollen cheek. Gwen looked over at her two closes family members, and knew right then that Ty and Little Tish was now two of a kind. She pulled up at the hospital emergency and they rushed in while Ty was carrying Little Tish in his arms and they rush up to the nurse's station.

"She's been shot!" Ty yelled at the nurse as they rushed around to assist them.

One of the nurse behind the counter said, "Do you have insurance Sir?"

"Of course the best, is Dr. Moore in?" Ty asked through his swollen lips.

"You mean Dr. Bob Moore?"

"The white old man with the playboy smile," Ty said.

"Yea that's him, do you want me to page him?" The nurse asked.

"Yes, tell him that Ty's here, Julian brother and it's an emergency!"

"O'kay Sir., just one minute," and the nurse picked up the phone and called the doctor.

Ty looked over at Gwen and said, "go call Lady-G and tell her what happened."

"O'kay baby!" Gwen said as she rushed over to the pay phone.

Three minutes later Dr. Moore was in the emergency room. He saw Ty and said, "Damn my man, what happen to you? Did the wife get mad again?" The doctor smiled in a joking manner, and him and Ty shared a laugh, as Ty grabbed his left side to subdue the pain.

"Oh, you're busted up pretty good huh! Ty shook his head yes! Don't worry big Boy, I got you! Nurse he's coming with me."

"He hasn't filled out his paperwork yet." The nurse muttered.

"Don't worry about it, I got everything under control."

"O'kay Doctor!"

"And can you send my sister up when she's finished," Ty asked?

"O'kay sir."

"Doctor, my girl got shot in the ass during this ordeal, and they rushed her to the back already, can you make sure that she's alright." Ty said as they walked in the back.

"Sure Ty, but first let me order some x-rays for you and get you some ice packs."

144

* * * *

G-Fly was driving on the freeway headed to Hollywood to have a late lunch when Lady-G received a page from Gwen with her emergency code printed after the number. She looked over at G-Fly and said, "It's Gwen and she put in her emergency code." Then she grabbed her cell phone and called the number.

"Hello!" What? Say no more, we're on our way." Lady-G hung up the phone and said, "I think that the safe spot got hit, and Little Tish got shot in the butt and Ty is beaten up real bad, they're at Martin Luther King hospital!"

"G-Fly got over and off the freeway, and jumped back on going in the hospital direction. "Are they alright?" Princess asked in a concern voice.

"I believe so! If she got shot in the butt, it shouldn't be life threatening. She said that Ty got beaten up, so he should be fine too," Lady-G reasoned.

G-Fly looked over at Lady-G and said, "Get Julian on the line!" And Lady-G went to dialing. She called straight to Julian's cell phone and he picked up on the first ring.

"Hello?"

"Hey Julian! G-Fly wants to holla at you!" Lady-G handed G-Fly the cell phone.

"Yo J, peep! We just got a call from Gwen, and it seems like the girls stash spot just got hit by some jackers. Tish got shot in the butt and Ty got beat up pretty bad. There at King Hospital and we're on our way there now, but I need you to go check out the spot and make sure that it's cleaned up good, then meet us at the hospital. O'kay! See you there!" Click!

G-Fly hung up, as his thoughts started analyzing the situation.

They arrived at the hospital within 15 minutes time and Gwen was waiting for them in the emergency waiting room. She quickly explained to them what Tish told her that happened during the jack move, and everybody was moved at the part of the story when Little Tish dove over Ty to shield him from being shot and killed. "Now that's a down little bitch!" G-Fly said.

"Yep that's my girl!" Princess said.

"Will ya'll take a bullet for a playa too?" G-Fly asked as he looked at Lady-G and Princess.

"Of course baby!" Lady-G said.

"You know that we will daddy." Princess said with a small giggle.

G-Fly looked at little G in his arms and said, "You can always tell when bitches lie son, just wait till they open their mouth!"

"Ooowww, you're scandalous! Don't tell him that." Lady-G said as everybody laughed.

"Look he's smiling, he knows that I ain't lying!" G-Fly said as he started laughing. G-Fly kissed his son and said, "Come on ya'll let's go see how our people is doing."

They walked in the back and seen Ty sitting in a chair with an ice pack on his right eye and on his lift cheek. Ty looked up and seen G-Fly and the ladies walking up and he took the ice pack off of his face and stood up." Damn nigga! Are you alright?" G-Fly asked as the girls gave him a hug and kiss.

"Yea, I'm cool! I got three cracked ribs and a fractured nose. But for the most part I'll live. Doctor Bob is in surgery taking out the bullet from Little Tish butt. He said that she should live but will need a whoopee' cushion for a while."

Everyone let out a heavy breath of relief. As Julian and Dee-Dee came off the elevator and headed in their direction.

"What's up Rad?" Julian said as he gave Ty their secret hand shake.

"Man They caught a brotha slippin and put a jack move down on us and almost killed me, but Little Tish jumped on top of me while I was unconscious, and shielded me from the shot. They shot her in the butt and left."

"Who was it?"

"Don't know, it happen so quick and I was unconscious through most of the jack move. The nigga just fucked me up out of spite, and then wanted to shot me just because! It couldn't be our other enemies, because I believe that they would've killed us both anyway. So it had to be someone who was just on to us and wanted to come up." Ty explained as Doctor Moore came walking in.

"Well, everything went well! We got the bullet out and sewed her up and she should be able to leave after her IV runs out. She lost a lot of blood so she would probably be weak until her blood stream reproduce. We wanted to give her a blood transfusion, but she refused it, so her body just has to replenish itself. We need you to fill out some forms and provide the nurse with your insurance information."

"O'kay doc we got you!" G-Fly said.

"Julian! It's really good to see that you've recovered so good and quickly. Usually, it would take months for a person to start walking around like this, and you did it in a few weeks. I'm proud of you!" Doctor Moore said, as everyone smiled and Julian looked at G-Fly and his eyes expressed his gratitude.

"Ty keep that ice pack on your face so the swelling will go down, and try not to lift any heavy objects. It will take a couple of months for your ribs to heal, and I've prescribed something to help you get through the pain."

"Gotcha Doc!" Ty said as Lady-G walked up with the hospital forms in her hand, then sat down and filled them out.

* * * *

"Yo cuz, this was a good lick." One of the jackers said as he counted the money with his other two Crimees.

"You ain't lying, I ain't never had this much money before...it's on and poppin now!" The other jacker said.

"I told ya'll that it was a sweet lick cuz. All ya'll got to do is ride with a nigga and it's on! I got a new connection that I'm about to get with, and we're going to have the whole eastside on lock.

"I'm feeling that cuz!"

"Me too nigga, I'm trying to get paid and lock this dope game down."

"Listen, ya'll can't be telling no one about this lick, because if them niggas find out that we we're behind this, then they're coming with guns smoken and they know how to put in work too! The niggas who set the lick up said.

"Man fuck them nigga cuz! He better be glad that I didn't smoke his punk ass and that little bitch too, I don't give a damn about them niggas, I'll bust my guns too!"

"That's right cuz! Fuck them busta's."

"I feel you, but keep this lick between us. It's $480 g's here, so that's $160,000 thousand dollars for both of ya'll and I hope ya'll stay low key with this money for a while. You know, let things cool down before ya'll start bussing fly whips and shit."

"O'kay cuz we will, ain't that right Ghost?"

"Yea, I'm chilled!"

"Cool, I'm out!"

Chapter 11
Looking Death In The Eye

Ty and Little Tish were at the main house laid up getting catered to like spoiled kids. The half of million dollars lost wasn't even an issue to the family, they were just happy that Ty and Little Tish made it out alive. Especially considering, the war that's been going on, and all of the blood that has been shed. G-Fly and Julian move the girls stash spot to another location that had bars on the doors. Then they expressed to the girls how important it was for them to be aware of their surroundings and make sure that they're not being followed after making the sale to their clients.

Because a nigga would buy some dope from them and have their home-boy or girl follow them back to the stash spot to get up on where they keep their money. Princess and the girls understood and promised to be more aware of their surroundings.

Later on that evening, Big Bro came by the main house to put the youngsters up on his surveillance on Felony.

"Listen, he lives alone and he be coming in and out a lot. I think that he might keep his work there because he be coming home at all hours of the day and night, and leaving within a few minutes carrying bags in and out. Here's some photos of him coming and going.

"Damn, he's a big ugly muthafucka!" G-Fly said as he passed the photo to Ty.

"Yep, that's the same nigga that Little Tish and Princess described." Ty said as he handed it to Julian.

"Now do you want me to snatch him or just kill him?"

"Well, it would be best to try to snatch him up, and see if we can get some information on Monster and Little Creep's where about," Julian said.

"That means that we might have to take him somewhere and torture him. Like to the stash house on Broadway. It got a big garage that was made sound proof for a music studio. We just never put no equipment back in it." Ty said as he remembered the old house that 'Game', their old mentor used as one of his safe house back in the day.

"O'kay I'll take Big Bro over there so we can get everything together. And then, we can catch him slippin and put it down."

"That sounds like a good plan to me, the sooner the better!" Ty said as everyone shook their head in agreement.

So how's Lil Momma coming along? Julian asked as he smiled and looked at Ty.

"She's doing fine! I got her running the business and she got the clientele picking up real good. She's been driving our clients around in the limo service, and they seem to like the presence of a beautiful lady. The other day she was driving this female movie actress around, and some hostile fan approached the actress aggressively, and she subdued him. Now she's getting calls from all over. She wanted to ride with me on the stake out, but I told her that I was cool and that I'll call her when I need her," Big Bro said.

"Good for her!" G-Fly said as he laughed.

"If she's doing good with the business then let her stay with that! If we really need her assistance, then we'll bring her in. But right now, I think that we can handle the hard part." Julian said to Big Bro as Big Bro shook his head yes...!

"O'kay, let's see how much Mr. Felony knows!" Ty said with an evil grin on his face.

* * * *

Wheels was sitting at the table across for Felony and Monster as they met up at the Red Lobster to discuss their business interest.

"So you say that you can move ten birds a week with no problem?"

"At least, and that's probably on a bad week."

"Well tell me, how have you been able to move this work without any problems from the youngsters, who suppose to have this territory on lock?" Felony asked.

"Listen, we ain't got to beat around the bush! I know that ya'll from Compton and it's obvious that ya'll are the one's who been warring with the youngster over their territory. You guys even shot up my dope spots a couple of times." Felony started easing his hand toward the butt of his gun as wheels was speaking. "And if I was working for the youngsters or wanted to set you up, you would already be dead! So you can take your hand off your gun, my business with ya'll is straight up and down. I use to work for the youngster running their blocks and dope houses, but when ya'll came warring at them, they got mad at me for going behind their backs and copping from some Mexicans to keep the dope spots running. So they ostracized me, and told me that I can keep the dope spots and dope street as a gift. But they refuse to sale me shit," Wheels stated.

"So you use to be a part of their little click." Felony asked wanting clarification.

"I sold work for them and held down their dope spots, but I didn't have nothing to do with ya'll beef!"

"How we know that you're not trying to cross us to get back in good with them?" Monster asked.

"Because you're still breathing, and plus; I just got through jacking one of their safe houses. I didn't appreciate the way they just used me as their mule, and then just kicked me to the curve like a bitch. So I followed one of their bitches to one of their spots, and sent my boys in there to hit them." Wheels consciously confessed.

"So you know where they live at," Monster asked?

"If I did, then I would've ran in on them and jacked them. But they're too smart for that! I had to deal with their bitches, and they only dealt with me through their pager. I called, and they will come and bring me my work – I'd give them their money and they leave.

"So can you call them now and buy some work," Felony asked?

Wheels looked at Monster then at Felony like he was crazy. "Listen player, if I could call them and order work, then I wouldn't be here talking to you! They all disaffiliated themselves from me, so now I'm looking for a new connection so I could get this money. It's either ya'll or the Southside Mexicans and I don't get down good with them bean eating muthafuckas. So I'm trying to see what ya'll trying to do, especially considering that ya'll might run this city in a minute." And they all started laughing.

"So you can't get us close to none of them," Monster asked?

"Not right now, but if I run into them somewhere then I can probably give you a call and let you catch up with them." Wheels suggested.

"Yea, that would be cool! And in the mean time, my man here will sell you whatever you can afford, but if you cross him, then I'll personally kill everything you love. Do you feel me cuz?" Monster threatened.

"Yeah, I feel you cuz...!" Wheels said.

Monster and Felony stood up and Felony said, "Meet me at the chicken spot on 53rd and Hoover in 20 minutes, and come alone," then they walked away.

When they got outside of the sea food restaurant Monster said, "Make sure that you don't let him know too much, he can't be trusted. He ain't got a loyal bone in his body. After he put us up on one of the bitch's where-abouts, then we'll kill his bitch ass."

Felony smiled at Monster and said "Gotcha," As they jumped into their cars and left.

* * * *

Princess, Gwen and Dee-Dee was all at the main mansion kicking it with Little Tish as she was getting pampered like a little doll.

"Look at you girl, you're acting spoil. Ty won't let her leave the house and she's laying around like she's a queen!" Gwen joked.

"I am a queen, bitch! I'm just a gangsta queen....like Cleopatra!" Tish said as her and Princess gave each other a high five.

"Yea, you're a bad bitch to jump in front of that bullet like that! What was going through your mind when you did that," Dee-Dee asked?

"I don't know girl, I just seen that nigga aim his gun at my Ty, and I just wanted to save him. He was

154

unconscious and I didn't want to see him die like that. That's my man and I vowed to kill and die for him, so I guess that my instincts just took over, and I tried to protect him."

"Ooowow, that's so sweet! I got to hand it to you girl, you're a down bitch!" Dee-Dee said.

"Shit we all should be down enough to jump in front of a bullet for our men, they took us in when we didn't have shit, and gave us more love then anyone ever did. Now you bitches got millions and can afford anything that you want. So you better be loyal and grateful to them, because without them, you hoes would probably be still fucked up running around selling $20 dollar rocks on the block, renting your pussy's to a suga-daddy for some crumbs." Princess scolded her crew.

"Shit bitch, who said that we ain't loyal to the cause? I just ain't never been in that kind of situation to prove my love like that, but if the situation cause for it, then I'ma ride and die with my men! Gwen said as Dee-Dee gave her a high five.

Lady-G walked in carrying Lil G and said, "Tish your man Ty wants you outside, he's in the front." Tish looked up then got up walking slow.

"Look at her, when her man Ty calls she gets her fat sore butt up and go see what he wants." Gwen joked as everyone followed her and started laughing with her.

"Fuck you guys! Tish muttered as she limped to the front door and opened it, and it was a brand new convertible 911 Porshe Carrera Turbo black on black with a big red bow waiting in the front driveway, with her name written on the window. The tow truck driver said, "Now which one of you lovely ladies is Ms. Tish."

"I am!" Tish said and he handed her the key to her new car and said, "Enjoy....!"

"Damn girl, I'm scared of you!" Princess said as everyone screamed with excitement.

Tish limped over to her new car and opened up the door, and a black suede box was laying on the driver seat. She picked it up and opened it, and a beautiful diamond bracelet was staring at her seducing her eyes with every sparkle.

"Damn, that bracelet is like that! Dee-Dee said as Tish blushed.

Tish sat in her new car and cranked it up, then revved the powerful engine and felt the power come alive. "Do you want to go for a drive," Lady-G asked?

"No not right now! I don't think that I can properly operate the clutch with this weak leg."

"O'kay baby, you can just leave it parked right here until you feel better. I guess that this is Ty's way of saying that he appreciates you!" Lady-G said as she smiled and bent down and kissed Tish on the forehead, then turned and walked back into the house.

"Princess, help me get out of this car....I'm stuck!" Tish said as everyone started laughing at her.

* * * *

It was later on that night and Big Bro was on the stake out with the youngsters at Felony's low key spot. Big Bro was in a camouflage out-fit that blended in with the bushes that was around Felony's driveway, and the youngsters were down the street in a dark blue Lincoln Continental town car. They were bent down low in the seats so their presence would stay undetected. They had an eagle view of Felony's driveway, but still couldn't identify where Big Bro was located. Big Bro was trained to lay on his prey for hours in the worse spaces and conditions known to man.

Felony hit the block in his Toyota rent a car and drove by the youngsters as he pulled into his driveway. He parked in back of his Cadillac and jumped out with his big 357 magnum clenched in his hand. He heard a low pop sound and looked down and seen wires attached sticking out of his stomach and chest, and instantly fell to the ground and started shaking as the taser gun sent twenty thousand volts through his body.

Felony's gun fell to the ground as his body collapsed under the electroshock that entered it. Big Bro went over and hand cuffed Felony as he was still shaking on the ground and he picked up Felony's gun and placed it in his waste band.

The youngsters saw Big Bro take Felony down with ease, and they laughed as they got out of the car and walked over to assist him.

Big Bro saw the youngsters walking over as he pulled the taser spikes out of felony's body taking bits of flesh along with it. "Damn, you fucked him up!" Ty said as Big Bro smiled and handed Ty Felony's keys.

Julian reached down and put some duck tape over Felony's mouth and then taped his legs together. "Let throw him in the trunk of his car!" Julian said and as they opened up the trunk they saw a duffle bag; they unzipped the bag and saw stacks of hundred dollar bills. Ty smiled and looked over at G-Fly and said, "Bingo!" They grabbed the duffle bag from the trunk and picked Felony's big ass up and throw him head first into the trunk of his car.

"Damn, this nigga must've shitted on himself! G-Fly said as he made a scrunch-up face.

"Come on ya'll, let's go check his house for his stash. Big Bro watch this nigga, and if he start acting up then taser his shitty ass again. And if someone comes up then taser them too." Ty said as the three youngsters laughed as they used Felony house key to enter his house. Ty was in the lead with his gun drawn as they entered Felony lavished three bedroom house. They all separated as they went through the house with their guns drawn looking in every room, making sure that Felony didn't have anyone staying in the house with him. "Clear!" Ty said as he exist the back room.

"I'm clear up front too!" Julian said.

"Hey ya'll, in here....jack pot!" G-Fly said as he stood in the guess bedroom staring into the closet.

Ty and Julian walked up and saw the kilos stacked on the floor of the closet, and they smiled. "Ya'll get the dope; I'll go check for the money." Julian said as he went into the other room.

Ty grabbed the blanket off the bed and laid it out on the floor, and started putting the dope in the blanket as they tied up the blanket, and carried the dope in it like that.

Julian met them in the front room with a big suit case and said "Found it!"

"Cool let's roll! We got other business to attend too! Ty said as they walked out.

Fifteen minutes later they were at the stash house on Broadway in the garage as they had Felony hand cuffed and gagged with duck tape looking up at his worse nightmare, and Big Bro and the three youngsters stared down at him.

"What's up Felony! Oh, you didn't think that we will catch up to your punk ass?" Julian asked as he pulled the duck tape from over his mouth pulling bits of skin off his lips with it. Felony made a low grunting sound.

"Listen player, we can do this the easy way, or the hard way, it's totally up to you!" G-Fly said.

"Man, ya'll might as well kill me because I don't got shit to say to ya'll!" Felony muttered as he looked up with a mean look in his eyes.

"O'kay, we can play it like that, but I want you to meet my big Brother. He's trained in all kinds of crazy torturous shit, and he can't wait to try it out on a tuff nigga like you. Now, we can give you a hundred g's and two of these keys, and let you leave this State and start a new life some where else. Or we can do it the other way, and you won't come out so pretty." G-Fly said with an ugly grin on his face.

"Cuz, I don't know who in the fuck you think that I am. I know that I'm gonna die, so you can save yourself some time, cause I already said my prayers." Felony expressed with a fearless look on his face.

"O'kay, have it your way! G-Fly looked at Big Bro and said, "He's all yours!"

Big Bro smiled as he looked down at Felony and Felony looked up at him and G-Fly stepped back to where Ty and Julian was, and lit a joint as they looked on wondering what Big Bro was going to do to Felony.

Big Bro pulled Felony up in a sitting position by his shirt, then kneeled down on one knee and wrapped is arm around Felony's neck in a chock hold, and started chocking him out as Felony helplessly gag for air while his hands was still hand cuffed behind his back rendering him defenseless.

"I always wanted to do that." Ty said as the youngsters looked on in amazement.

"Oh shit, he's going to kill him!" Julian said as he looked on.

"Yep his eye's is getting low! Look, he's out! Damn, this crazy nigga killed him! How we suppose to get some information out of his punk ass now?" G-Fly looked at Julian and Ty for some sort of understanding, as Big Bro let Felony's body drop to the ground, and then he started beating on Felony's chest.

"This muthafucka went crazy! G-Fly said as he put his hand on the butt of his 45 automatic. Big Bro took out his taser and shot Felony in the stomach with it, then blow into his mouth three times, and hit his chest three more times and Felony eyes shot open and he grasp for air as he started breathing hard and looking around in shocked.

"Now that was some crazy shit!" Ty said as he hit the joint again and passed it to G-Fly.

"You ain't bullshitting that was some straight terrorist shit!" Julian muttered.

"Welcome back from the dead nigga! Do you want to talk now, or should we send your tuff ass back to hell a couple of more times." G-Fly asked as he looked down at Felony grasping for air. "The devil must got this nigga tongue, send him back!" G-Fly said as Big Bro grabbed Felony by the shirt again.

"Wait, wait, O'kay – O'kay man what ya'll want to know? Felony screamed.

"Where do Monster live at," G-Fly asked?

"Man I don't know, he don't let no one know where he lives."

"He's lying!" Julian said from across the room.

"I ain't lying, he'd be a fool to let anyone know where he lives at."

"You got to know something – either save your life or save his!" G-Fly firmly said.

"O'kay, O'kay, he brought his baby momma a beauty salon that's on Long Beach Blvd. It's called Fly Girls!"

"What's her muthafucken name?"

"It's Brenda!"

"What about that nigga Little Creep, where do he live," Julian asked?

Felony eyes got big by the mention of Lil Creep name.

"Oh, you didn't think that we knew about that nigga huh?" G-Fly said with a ugly laugh.

"Man, I don't know where that nigga lives – nobody do, but probably that nigga Monster."

"Miss me nigga, you got to know something about him, where his bitch work or something?" Julian said.

"Not that I can think of!"

"Well nigga you better start thinking harder if you want to save your own ass." G-Fly said as Felony looked at G-Fly then at Big Bro.

"O'kay man, his son goes to Compton High school! He's one of the star running backs for the football team. Felony confessed as he shook his head in shame.

"I think he's lying!" Ty said.

"Listen man, I ain't got no reason to lie to ya'll. I've told ya'll everything I know. I was just sent out here to sell some work. I didn't have anything to do with ya'll war."

"Oh you didn't huh?" G-Fly asked as Felony shook his head in his defense.

"So that wasn't you who pulled up on me at the light in the Monte Carlo trying to kill me! And you didn't have anything to do with gunning down my brother here and killing is fiancée and unborn child." Felony eyes started to water because he knew that the inevitable was coming. "Normally, we'd go kill everything you love from your seeds to that crazy bitch who had you. But for the assistance that you gave us today, we're going to spare them."

"I appreciate it." Felony mumbled.

"But it's up to my man here," and G-Fly pointed at Julian, "he's going to decide what your fate is going to be. You had his fiancée and baby killed, and I think that he's fucked up about that! It's all your's J."

G-Fly stepped back as Julian started to slowly approach Felony on the floor.

"I'm sorry man!" Felony cried.

Julian looked at him and said, "I know," and raised the 9mm with the silencer attached to it and unloaded the whole clip into Felony's face and chest.

"Damn this nigga always likes to make a big mess! I'll go grab some towels and blankets out of the house," Ty said as

G-Fly and Big Bro laughed and Julian reached down and grabbed Felony's pager off his belt and checked it.

"Hey Fly, do this number look familiar to you?" Julian asked as he gazed at the number on the beeper.

G-Fly walked over and looked at the number and said, "Your muthafucken right it do, that's Wheels number! I told you that we should've killed his punk ass. Now look, he was plotting to take us out all along." G-Fly said as he paced back and forth.

Ty walked in with the towels and blankets and G-Fly said, "Ty you'll never believe what we ran across?"

Ty looked at G-Fly then at Julian and said, "What?"

"Wheels muthafucken home number was on Felony beeper."   G-Fly uttered.

"What? You're bullshitting….let me see." Julian showed him the number.

"Yep, that's that niggas' number alright!" Ty said as he shook his head.

"What you think J?"

"OH, his ass is dead!"

G-Fly, Ty and Big Bro started laughing. "I been told your ass that we should've killed him, we don't know how much shit that he could've told these fools. We got to warn Princess and the girls, so they won't get caught slippin if they run across him before we do."

G-Fly pulled out his cell phone as Julian, Ty and Big Bro started cleaning up the mess, and wrapping up Felony's dead body.

They disposed of the dead body, bloody rags, and dirty gun, and a couple of hours later they where at the other stash spot counting their spoils of war, "Check it out!" Ty said, we got $680,000 thousand dollars and 52 keys. That's a $170,000 thousand dollars and 13 keys a piece. Now considering that Big Bro is not in the drug distribution business," Ty looked over at Big Bro and smiled, "It's only right that we pay him for his share of the dope to keep it 100%! So, we'll give you 10g's off every kilo, and that would bring your share of the cut to $300,000 thousand dollars, fair enough?"

"Hell yea, that's love!" Big Bro said as everyone laughed and gave each other a ghetto hand shake.

"Well, let's set a meeting for tomorrow at two o'clock in the evening," Julian said.

"O'kay, do you want me to bring little Momma," Big Bro asked?

"No, let her continue dealing with the legitimate business aspect. Here give her this," and Julian throw Big Bro a $5,000 thousand dollar stack of bills, "and tell her that we think that she's doing a wonderful job."

"O'kay, what ever you guys say!"

Julian looked over at Ty and said, "Tell the girls to come and get this work tomorrow and take it to their stash spot."

"Gotcha."

"Tonight was a good night, but we still got a lot more work to do before this is over, so stay focused and keep your gun cocked and ready to blast." Julian said as they grabbed their money and left out.

Chapter 12
The Cross

It was the 9:15a.m. the next morning and Monster was at Felony's low key house pacing back and forth in the living room waiting on Felony to arrive. Monster spoke to Felony yesterday and made plans to pick up the money that Felony already made and transport it to the safe house in Compton, so Little Creep could pick it up and take it to his private stash spot. Monster was getting pissed as he waited for Felony to arrive.

"This nigga know how I feel about being delayed like this!" Monster said to himself as he decide to just go get the money out of the bedroom closet and just take it with him, and get with Felony later when he gets home and realize that the money's gone.

Monster laughed at his scandalous thoughts and walked into Felony's bedroom to retrieve the money. When he got to the closet it was already wide open, but no suit case or duffle bag was in sight. He started moving things around in the closet but still no money, so he went into the other bedroom where they kept the dope and when he open the closet, his heart skipped a beat as he seen Felony's dead body looking mangled and his whole face was nearly shot off.

Monster instantly pulled his gun out as his mind started to race then he grabbed a face towel and wiped everything down on his way out of the door. He jumped in his car and grabbed his cell phone as he drove away.

"Hello!" The voice on the other end of the phone said.

"We got a problem," Monster said into the phone.

"What kind of problem?"

"Our main man is down and everything that he had is gone." Monster said.

"Damn, everything?"

"Yep everything!"

"Did you see him?"

"Yep, what's left of him."

"O'kay, meet me at your spot in an hour."

"I'm on my way." Click, Monster hung up the phone and jumped on the freeway as he looked in his rear view mirror to see if any-one was following him.

* * * *

Wheels just got through dropping off his dope sacks to his workers and rock houses, when he made a stop by the liquor store in his hood to grab him some Hennessy and New Port cigarettes, when a big figure walked up on side of him and order a pack of Camels cigarettes and a 7up. Wheels looked to his side and saw Monster and said "Hey big man, what's good?" With a pleasant smile on his face.

Monster was looking in Wheels eyes for any signs of deceit and detected none. "Nothing at all player, is it possible I can have a moment of your time?"

"Sure, my cars parked right outside." Wheels said as he noticed one of Monsters homies standing right in back of him. They started walking out and Wheels asked, "Is there a problem big man?"

"Naw, you're cool little bro....I just need some answers." Monster said as they jumped in Wheels rent a car and Monster homie got in the back seat.

Wheels didn't like the vibes that he was getting but knew if it was something serious with him, then Monsters approach would've been a whole lot different. "So what's on your mind," Wheels asked?

"Did you hook up with Felony yesterday?"

"Yeah, we hooked up and he brung me ten like we discussed."

"Did he say anything else to you?"

"Not really, he just said to call him as soon as I see the youngster or their girls, and for me to page him when I need something. Why, what's up?"

"Well he got killed the other night and we're trying to trace his moves." Monster said as he looked Wheels in the eyes to see if he can detect any type of foul play or lies.

"Damn, my condolences cuz! The nigga was good when he left me. Do you think that the youngsters killed him?"

"It's a possibility, but I don't have no proof."

"OH shit, today must be your lucky day cuz!" Wheels uttered as Monster looked at him then at what he was looking at.

That's one of the youngster's bitches....that's Gwen! She push weight for the youngsters."

"Monster eyes got big, then he looked back at his homie Trouble and said, "Go start the car and park next to her car, we're going to snatch this bitch." Then he looked at Wheels and said, "I'll catch up with you later, good lookin-out cuz!"

"Handle your business cuz! And you better not sleep on that bitch," Wheels yelled.

Gwen stopped by the liquor store to grab her some snacks to feed her weed craving. She just dropped off $240,000 thousand dollars at the new stash spot and was taking her $30,000 thousand dollar profit to where her and the girls keep their personal stash. As she was walking back up to the car she was approached by a big ugly swoll nigga who was dressed nice. "Excuse me Ms. Can I have a moment of you time?" Monster said as he walked up to Gwen.

"Well I'm kind of in a hurry right now." Gwen said as she kept walking in stride.

The man caught up with her and said, "It would only take a minute," and Gwen stopped by her car and turned toward the big man as Monster socked her right on the chin and knocked her out cold. Monster grabbed her purse from around her shoulder then picked her up and put her in the back seat of his Buick Regal, and jumped in the back with her as Trouble drove off.

Wheels made a scandalous smile as he saw Monster pull off with Gwen kidnapped in the back seat. "The shit just hit the fan!" Wheel said to himself as he laughed and drove off.

* * * *

Everybody was sitting around the round table waiting for the meeting to begin. G-Fly looked over at Princess and said, "Did you page her."

"Yeah baby I paged her twice. She must be in traffic or on her way," Princess said.

"O'kay, we'll just have to start without her.... Julian why don't you begin." G-Fly said as he looked over at his comrade.

"Well everyone knows what's going on so we might as well cut to the chase, and Princess you and the girls can fill Gwen in later.

We've successfully defeated majority of our enemies. Now we just got to take the heads out and we got a pretty good line on them that seem to check out. But we got to be very discreet with our approach, because the people that we're up against seem to be very wealthy in the game, and have a bunch of idiots on their team. They're gang members so their loyalty is motivated by a different type of impulses. Some is strong, some is weak, some is down and some is just along for the profits. Nevertheless, if we kill the head then they would loose their motivation and die off. They're weak without their leader, so our aim is to take out the head man and let his homies steal and run away with his wealth. Now we know where one of the dudes baby mamma work's at, and we know where the head man kid goes to school at, so we need to move swift and smart, and use these two people to our advantage.

Hopefully, they can lead us to the main source and we can put an end to this war once and for all," and everyone started clapping and shaking their heads yes, in agreement.

＊ ＊ ＊ ＊

Gwen was tide to a chair with her hands and feet bounded and a rag in her mouth with a torn cloth tide around her head to hold the rag in place. Her jaw was swollen and bruised and it felt like it was broken from the punch. She opened up her eyes and saw the big man who had approached her at the liquor store looking at her from across the room.

"I'm glad to see that you're awake, I thought that my punch killed you!" Monster and Trouble laughed at his sick sense of humor. You and your people has been very violent and disrespectful toward us, and you better hope that you're worthy of their devotion or this will be your last day on earth." A tear rolled down her cheek, because she knew that she was about to die.

169

She heard a knock on the door and another man walked in. The big guy whispered something in his ear and then he walked over to Gwen and slapped the mess out of her. Little Creep said "Listen bitch, I ain't got time for games. Either you tell me what I want to know, or I will torture you in everyway that is imaginable. Do you hear me?"

Gwen just looked at him with a blank facial expression, so he slapped her again and said, "Do you hear me?" She shook her head; yes!

Little Creep took off her gag and said, "Where do these young niggas live?"

"If you're looking for a ransom, then I'll give you a number that you can call and they'll give you anything that you want, but if you want me to betray them, then you might as well kill me now, because I'll never do that." Gwen firmly stated.

Little Creep looked at Monster and said, "No wonder why we're losing this war, these bitches are brainwashed. What's the muthafucken number bitch?"

The youngsters were going over their plans to get at Little Creep and Monster when the phone rang. Lady-G answered it,

"Hello!"

"Yea, let me speak to Julian."

"Who's calling?"

"Tell him it's Little Creep!"

"Lady-G got quite then said, "Please hold on a second." Lady-G waved her arm wildly at Julian to get his attention as everyone looked in her direction.

"It's Little Creep," Lady-G whispered in a high pitch voice.

Julian looked at Ty and G-Fly then grabbed the phone and said, "What a pleasant surprise….what do I owe the pleasure?"

"Oh, I see that you're on top of your game."

"Yea, your name came up in a few conversations. How did you get my number?"

"From your bitch here, Gwen I believe her name is!"

"What is it you want?" Julian said as he made a silent whisper with his lips and said, "He got Gwen," to everyone who was listening in on the conversation.

"Well since I believe that you just jacked my spot and left Felony behind, it's only right that I add that loss to your new bill along with Ms. Thang here, and I say that three million dollars should be a adequate amount to compensate me for my losses and troubles."

"O'kay, where do you want to meet at for the exchange, and I expect a far exchange the paper for the bitch," Julian said.

"I ain't got no problem with that! But if you try anything crazy then I'ma blow this bitch head clean off."

"I feel you nigga, but let me speak to her to make sure that she's still alive.

"Ha, ha, ha, here bitch say what's up to your man."

"Hey daddy!"

"Are you alright?"

"Yea, just a little scared!"

"Don't worry I'm coming to get you o'kay!"

"That's enough nigga, I'll call you back in an hour with the location, have the money ready and no games or the next time you see this bitch will be at her funeral. Click!"

The phone went dead in Julian's ear as he hung up the phone then looked up at his crew and said, "They got Gwen, and they're asking for three million dollars for the trade."

"Baby we got some money saved," said Princess.

"Don't worry baby, money ain't the issue! They'll be calling us back in an hour to tell us where the meeting place will be. Now nine times out of ten, it will be a set up, so we got to be ready for the big dance. Big Bro call Lil Momma and I want you and her here on deck and ready for everything."

"I'm on it." Big Bro said as he turned and walked out.

"Ty, you go get the paper! Ty shook his head and walked out. G-Fly said, "I got a plan! I'll be back." Then he turned and walked out too.

"Princess, you and Dee-Dee go strap up and make sure that ya'll put on your bullet proof vest."

"O'kay baby!" Princess said as she gave Lil Tish and Lady-G a kiss and a hug as they ran out."

Lady-G and Lil Tish looked up at Julian, hoping that he would allow them to participate in the plan and Julian sensed their hunger and looked over at them as they stared at Julian like two puppies looking for a snack, and Julian said, "I need you both to be my eyes and ears. You'll be parked down the street, and if shit gets heated, then I need ya'll to be around to make sure that nobody is left behind stranded or hurt. This doesn't mean that you can participate in the shoot out, we need you two out just in case we get busted or fall victim to the game. I'm sure that you two can handle the businesses if we should fail, or loose this battle. So understand your position and try to stay invisible out there. I want ya'll to wear bullet proof vests just in case." Then Julian gave them a stern stare and walked away.

It took 45 minutes for everyone except G-Fly to be dress for war. Julian looked around at everyone then stood up and started to speak.

"Listen, everyone here today has an important choice and decision to make, lives' will be taken, blood will be shed, if we get caught the penalty is death or a life sentence in the Prison.

This is a critical decision that you must make. These niggas got our sister hostage and I doubt if they did it for the money, because their whole objective has been to kill us and take away our territory. So I believe that blood is the only ransom that they're looking for, so blood and death is what we're paying them with. Our first priority is to get our sister back. And if we're successful at handling this, then will kill everything that poses a threat to us. If we can't get her back, then we'll make sure that her death wasn't in vain.

Now that you know what's required of you and the consequences of it, you have a serious choice to make. You can take your wealth and material gain and walk away now, and no harm or pain will come to you. Or you can stay with your family and fight to defend what we love, stand for, and believe in. The decision is yours to make now!"

Everyone looked around the table but no one moved. "Well, I guess that everyone chooses to ride!" And each person screamed and shouted with a simultaneous roar!

G-Fly walked in and smiled as he bent down and whispered in Julian ear.

That's right my nigga....that's the shit I'm talking about!" Julian said as he looked at his comrades and gave them the news as the phone rang.

"Hello!" Julian said.

"Get off the freeway on Wilmington and go east toward the railroad tracks. You'll see a blue Iroc sitting in front of an old warehouse and bring the money." Click! The phone went dead.

"He wants us to meet him down at some warehouse in Compton. It's straight down Wilmington across the railroad tracks. A blue Iroc is supposed to be parked in front of it."

"Listen, don't let him lure you inside of the warehouse, that will be to his advantage and most likely will be a trap. Bring him out, so we can get a visual on him and his crew, and me and Lil Momma will pick them off like fish in a barrel."

"O'kay, go find a spot and lay low and don't forget that it's in Sheriff area so watch your backs, they shoot then ask question later."

"Me too!" Big Bro said as him and Lil Momma grabbed their walkie-talkies that was programmed to everyone else's, and got up and left.

"Ty, I want you to be my driver! G-Fly you stay around 30 yards in back of us with the package. Princess and Dee-Dee, I want ya'll to watch G-Fly's back, but stay 20 yards away from him at a angle to defend against whatever shooter that may try to come up behind ya'll. Lady-G, you and Tish play the scene from a distance, so you can assist if anyone get hurt or needs your aid. I want ya'll to be in the Chevy F-10 Track so if someone gets trapped they can just jump in the back of the bed as you drive. Make sure that ya'll keep an eye out for the ghetto bird. We need to try to be in and out before the Sheriff's make it on the scene, because we can't win in court if we're caught at the scene, but if you get stopped away from the crime scene and get searched on suspicion, then we can possible beat it in trail. So stay on your game, and watch each other backs, and shoot to kill. A toast to the family," and everyone held up their glass of Hennessy, and downed the liquor then they kissed and hugged each other before they left.

Chapter 13
Revenge Is Mine

Ty and Julian pulled up to the entrance of the warehouse and heard a voice call over the walkie-talkie say, "I got visual LB." Big Bro whispered as he used the initials of what he called them Little Bro.

"Good BB, LM are you home yet?" Julian asked as he held the button to the walkie-talkie down, then released it and heard Lil Momma say, "Yes daddy I'm home, and its two cars with six kids playing down the street."

"O'kay LM, PD stay on point." Julian whispered.

"Gotcha!" Princess said in reply as Ty pulled up into the warehouse lot and stopped 30 yards away from the big door, and G-Fly pulled up 20 yards in back of Ty and Julian in his White Blazer truck. Princess pulled right into the warehouse lot too, and parked right at the entrance way so she could see anything coming, and still keep a good eye on G-Fly as well as Ty and Julian.

The warehouse big garage door slid open and Ty and Julian saw three cars parked inside, with ten people standing around the cars. A big black nigga stepped up and waved Ty and Julian inside, as they both just stepped out of Ty's black Cadillac and Julian said, "Where's my girl at?"

A little man walked up smiling with another man on side of him holding a rope that was tide to Gwen's neck, and a double barrel shot gun in his other hand aimed at Gwen's back. "So you're the young muthafuckas who's been killin all of my homeboys." Little Creep said as he threw a mean look at Ty and Julian.

"You can say that! But truthfully we just protect what's ours and we don't believe in ducking no Rec!" Julian said as he gave an evil smile to Little Creep and Monster and they gave an evil look back with their eyes brows squinted.

"Is that right? Well nigga it's going to cost you to play this game. Did you bring my muthafucken money?"

"Of course! But I also bought something better. Then Julian waved his hand up and down and G-Fly got out of his Chevy mini Blazer with a AK-47 in his hands, then went around to the back passenger side door and pulled out Little Creep's son, who was hand cuffed behind the back with his legs in shackles.

Julian and Ty smiled as they both reached into the car and Julian pulled out an AR-15, and Ty pulled out two Mac 10's with extended clips then they both laughed and Ty said, "Check Mate!"

"Damn, they got Jr! Them son of bitches kidnapped my muthafucken son!" Little Creep yelled as he looked at Monster. Gwen started laughing as she watched Little Creep lose his composure.

"So how do you want to do this nigga? You got something that belongs to me and I got something that belongs to you. Either we all can die right here right now, or we can make this trade and catch up with each other later." Julian said as he spoke loud enough so every one could hear. Little Creep homeboys started looking around at each other because they knew that the script just flipped.

"O'kay nigga you did that, send my boy and I'll send your bitch!"

"Yea right! I'll tell you what, let my girl go so she can start walking this way, and we'll let your boy go so he can walk toward you. That way, if there's any funny shit, then we'll fill this little nigga up with holes." Julian said.

"O'kay every thing is cool, just let my boy go and we can make a fair trade. Every one hold your fuckin fired, nobody better not even think about shooting." Little Creep said as he looked over at his homeboy that had the rope that was around Gwen's neck and said, "Let her funky ass go!"

Gwen looked at Little Creep with death in her eyes as she started walking toward Julian, and Little Creep son started walking too, but the leg shackles prevented him from moving as fast as he struggled against the pain, and walked as fast as he could. As Gwen made it to Julian, Little Creep's son was just passing them up and Julian said, "Get in the back and keep your head down." Gwen hurried up and jumped in the back and Ty looked over at Julian and they both smiled and started unloading their guns into the crowd.

Little Creep said, "Nooo, as his son got gun down by the Mac 10 bullets and fell to the ground. "Kill them," Little Creep yelled as he dove on the ground and pulled out two 9mm and started busting as he rolled for cover.

Two niggas ran out; one with a rocket launcher and the other with an AK-47 and as soon as they aimed, two silent bullets whistled through the air and caught both of the men in motion. One got hit in the forehead and the other one got hit in the left eye, knocking both of their brains through the back of their heads.

Monster pulled out his Mac 10 from under his coat and got hit twice in the chest area by Ty's Mac 10 as he sprayed wildly side to side. The bullet knocked Monster off his feet and saved him from getting hit by

Julian's AR-15 bullets, as the nigga who was running up behind Monster big ass got hit three times, and the bullet dropped him and he was dead before he hit the ground.

G-Fly was using his driver side door for support as he unloaded rounds from his Ak-47 into the garage.

Princess had a 45 automatic and Dee-Dee had two 9mm that they were bussin' into the garage. Two cars pulled up out of no where, and six niggas jumped out with AR-15, 12 gages, Mac10's and big caliber hand guns, and started bussin' at Princess and Dee-Dee.

The first two who had the two AR-15 assault riffles dropped as soon as they jumped out of the car. The one with the 12 gage and Mac 10 got off a couple of rounds before they got shot in the back of the head. One of the men said, "they got snipers on the roofs," and he got shot as the other one tried to run around to the other side of the car, only to get shot down by Princess and Dee-Dee as they turned their attention on the two cars that pulled up.

Little Creep rolled over to his dead homie and grabbed his AK-47 riffle and started unloading it at Ty and Julian as a bullet went through the car door and hit Ty on the side of his leg, and he fell to one knee then pulled himself into the car as Julian reloaded his AR-15, and jumped up and caught Little Creep as he ran out of bullets and got caught standing with an empty gun, Julian unloaded his new clip into Little Creeps body nearly chopping him in half.

"Daddy," Little Creep son said, as Julian pulled out his 45 automatic and aimed it at the boy, and Monster jumped up bussin' his Mac 10 into Julian's bullet proof vest knocking Julian to the ground. Then Monster got hit twice by two silent bullets, one in the forehead and the other in the chest; killing him instantly.

G-Fly ran over and helped Julian up and carried him to the car and threw him in the backseat with Gwen, then he jumped into the driver seat and started to drive off when he saw Little Creep's son crawling over toward his father's dead body.

G-Fly then pointed his AK-47 out the window and shot six rounds into the boy's body, then drove in reverse over to Princess and Dee-Dee and said, "Go drive my truck," and Dee-Dee ran and jumped in the Mini Blazer and pulled around, just as a sheriff car skidded to a stop 20 yards from the entrance to the warehouse lot, and two policemen jumped out of their vehicle with their guns drawn, as two silent bullets flew through the air and entered their heads killing them both dead, leaving them twisted in the street.

G-Fly punched the gas peddle and the Cadillac lead the way down the street hitting corners, as they drove down side streets making a get away. G-Fly finally pulled over after ten blocks, and grab the guns from Gwen and took them to Princess car, then after making sure Julian was alright he took him and put him in the car with Dee-Dee and they all pulled-off and went separate ways.

Lady-G and Little Tish picked up Lil Mamma as she climbed down from the roof top of the building across from the warehouse. As they were driving away they saw two sheriff police cars pull to a stop right in front of Big Bro's undercover bucket.

Big Bro didn't wasted any time as he jumped out with two 45 automatic and started shooting at the police.

The first two police got caught slipping as Big Bro shot one in the head and the other one got shot in the face penetrating both sides of his jaw and knocking him out cold. The other two sheriffs jumped behind their door and started shooting it out with Big Bro.

"Here Lil Momma, you and Tish get ready to shoot." Lady-G said, as she gave Lil Momma her 357 magnum and pulled the Chevy F-10 truck right in back of the sheriff car, when the sheriff looked back, Lil Momma and Little Tish unloaded their guns into them, and shot them dead. Big Bro jumped back into his bucket and sped-off in back of Lady-G, as soon as they hit the corner Lady-G pulled over and Big Bro ran and jumped into the truck with the girls and squatted down on the floor board. Lady-G drove off and turned onto a main street as she saw a sheriff vehicle race by them on the opposite side of the street, Lady-G's heart beat echoed through the truck as she drove onto the freeway.

* * * *

Everybody met up at the safe house and it was all smiles and hugs. The bullet that hit Ty went straight through, so they took him to an old friend that Lady-G knew who was a retired RN, she cleaned him up and sewed up his wound and Ty was as good as new. G-Fly, Princess, and Gwen went to dispose of the cars and the weapons then everyone met back up at the main mansion at 8 o'clock that night.

Everyone was cleaned up and dressed up looking nice. The youngsters had everyone seated around the round table as Lady-G and Princess served everyone a glass of Louise the XIII and Crystal Champagne. Everyone was laughing and joking with one another as Julian looked at his watch and cut on the news.

The shoot out was all over the news station, and at the bottom of the screen the words was displayed, "Five sheriffs dead and one wounded in a gang related shoot out!"

The police detained a bum who lived in the warehouse and witnessed the whole shoot out. Julian looked at his crew as everyone was silently listening to the TV news broadcast and said, "I don't have to tell you guy's how serious this situation is. One peep of this gets out to the wrong ears, then we all can be facing the death penalty or forever in prison. Now we held our own, and fought to protect what is ours and a part of us." Julian then gazed at Gwen as Princess grabbed her hand and gently squeezed it. "And that's what family do. The Kennedy's did it, the Rockefeller's did it, and everyone before them who successfully built an empire did it! It's the American way, and the way of the world, so don't ever be ashamed of being a gansta. It's our heritage! Now from what I can tell we're looking pretty good on the safe part, if anything should arise behind this incident, then it would be purely circumstantial. So don't ever get scared into killing yourself by trying to justify anything if the police should come knocking at our door. We got a team of well educated attorneys for that.

Now on the other note, we have a potential problem that's still out there running wild, and we must take care of him before he becomes a serious threat. He's knows too much, therefore, he must die. I want Wheels dead within the next 24 hours and I hope that you girls can handle this easy tasked.

"We got him daddy," Princess said.

"O'kay, now for our new brother and sister we got a small surprise to show a token of our love, respect, and appreciation." Julian then handed them both an envelope with their names written on it. They opened it up and inside was a bank book from a Swiss bank account, they both looked inside their bank book and inscribed in it was the amount of $250,000 thousand dollars. "We got to always have an exist plan, and the worlds too big to stay in one spot, so after we clean up some loose ends, we're going to take a trip to Jamaica and spend a couple of weeks of pleasure." Each member began clapping and verbally expressed their excitement. "We got a long night ahead of us and Cindy prepared for us a feast to enjoy, so let's put an end to the past and look forward to a new future."

* * * *

Wheels was in his new condo watching the news and an eerie thought went through his mind. He cut up the TV and the news broadcaster said, "A horrible gang shoot out took place today at an undisclosed location in Compton California, that left five police sheriff's dead and one fatally wounded as well as fourteen known Compton gang members. The detectives have not disclosed as of yet, any answers to the deadly shooting, but it is assumed that it was drug related and the rival gang has fled the scene of the crime. A report has just come in and one of the dead gang members have been identified as Mark Porter aka Little Creep, the Compton kingpin."

"Damn, those little crazy muthafuckas' pulled it off!" Wheels said to himself. Then thought about it and said, "them crazy muthafuckas' fucked off my new connection. Damn, I can't win for losing!" Wheels mumbled as he checked his pager and seen that it was his dope spot number and smiled at how fast it sold out. He picked up the phone and called the number back.

"Hello, Yea! Damn that was quick! O'kay, I'm on my way."

* * * *

The following night Princess came up with a plan to catch Wheels slippin. Her and the girls drove around and handed out twenty dollar bills to smokers around Wheels dope house, and they happily accepted with no question asked. They handed out fifteen hundred dollars in twenties, and just laid back in the cut and waited for Wheels to arrive.

Wheels pulled up to his dope house on the eastside of Los Angeles with the butt of his 9mm clenched in his hand and tucked inside of his waste band, as he jumped out of his new 5.0 convertible Mustang. He walked in the dope spot and exchanged the money for the rock cocaine with his worker old man fox. He laughed and joked for a few and this smoked out lady that he knew approached him.

"Hey Wheels, can I holla at you?"

"What do you want Sandy?"

"Let me get some credit until the first? You know that I'm good for it."

"Bitch you know that I don't give no credit." Wheels said as he looked at the smoker lady like she was stupid.

"Come on Wheels, how about I give you some head then for a $20 dollar rock."

"Wheels looked at the smoked out lady up and down and said, Naw, I'm cool... I'll pass! You look like you'll give a dick VD just by suckin it." He started laughing and walked away.

"Fuck you nigga," the smoker said and left out of the door behind Wheels to see if she can go come up on a trick so she can get some money.

Wheels walked out the house and turned right to go get in his car and he heard a familiar voice say, "nice car and he turned around and saw Dee-Dee standing on the other side of the street and Wheels didn't even think twice as he pulled his gun out and started bussin' at Dee-Dee, as Dee-Dee ducked behind the park car and bullets rattled the side of the car. Wheels shot six shots and saw a movement from the car in front of him and he turned and saw Princess and started bussin' wildly at her as she ducked down behind the car and someone in back of him said, "Hey nigga!" Wheels turned and saw Gwen and started shooting at her as his 9mm ran out of bullets, and all of the girls came out with their guns drawn on Wheels.

Wheels broke and took off running as the first two shots hit him in the legs and he fell face down in the middle of the street.

Princess, Dee-Dee and Gwen circled around him then he turned and looked up at Princess as she said, "I told you that I'd kill you if you ever crossed the family."

Wheels unable to do anything smiled and spit on her foot, and with that all three girls pumped lead into Wheels' body.

Princess then put her shoe to Wheels' face and wiped the spit off, "You cock sucken-muthafucka' never disrespect a Princess; then all three girls hurried to their car and jumped inside and drove off.

Sandy was hiding behind a park car and saw Princess and the girls' gun down Wheels. After they had drove off Sandy ran over to Wheels bullet-riddled body and knelled down beside his blood soaked body. Wheels with his last breath looked up at her and said, "Help me!" In a low voice.

"O'kay, Sandy said; but first let me help myself before I help you! Then she reached into his pocket and took the two big wads of hundred dollar bills that he had, she reached around and grabbed his arm and took off his Rolex gold watch, bracelet, and diamond ring. "Now I'll go call for help."

Sandy ran away as wheels stared up at the sky and the sound of sirens started echoing in his ears, as it got dimmer, and dimmer and his eyes slowly closed.

Princess and the girls made it to the safe house without any problems. She picked up the cell phone and called the main house as G-Fly answered. "What's good?" G-Fly said as he answered the phone.

"Hi daddy, we made it back from the trip, and we had fun. I gave your friend her birthday present, and it knocked her dead. So where going to shower and clean up and we'll come by after we finish."

"O'kay beautiful, I see you then!" G-Fly said, as he hung up the phone and took the joint from Julian and said, "Wheels is dead!" With that the three youngsters' held up their glasses to give a silent toast "to the homie's who didn't make it, and to the ones who did…!"

THE END

Ghetto Theory Publishing

**Available January 2014,
The coldest West Coast tail every told.**

**LOOK FOR *G. PRINCE* LATEST NEW
RELEASES IN BOOK STORES AND FOR
PURCHASE ON AMAZON.COM**

COMING SOON GHETTO GAMES III

Ghetto Theory Publishing

Presents

Ghetto Games

Natural Born Gangster

Am I My Sister's Keeper?

**Rules of the Street Game that Every Hustler
Should Know...!**